JACK AT THE HELM

Also by Lisa Doan

The Berenson Schemes #1:
Jack the Castaway

The Berenson Schemes #2:
Jack and the Wild Life

SALIDA

JACK AT THE HELM

By Lisa Doan

illustrations by
Ivica Stevanovic

MINNEAPOLIS

Darby Creek
A division of Lerner Publishing Group, Inc.
241 First Avenue North
Minneapolis, MN 55401 USA

For reading levels and more information, look up this title at
www.lernerbooks.com.

Cover and interior images © iStockphoto.com/subjug (mail envelope);
© Christian Mueringer/Dreamstime.com (vintage postage stamp);
© iStockphoto.com/blondiegirl (postage meter); © ilolab/Shutterstock.com
(wood background); © Picsfive/Shutterstock.com (notepaper); © CWB/
Shutterstock.com (passport stamps); © Tsyhun/Shutterstock.com (canvas
passport background).

Main body text set in Janson Text LT Std 12/17.5.
Typeface provided by Linotype AG.

Library of Congress Cataloging-in-Publication Data

Doan, Lisa.
        Jack at the helm / by Lisa Doan ; illustrations by Ivica Stevanovic.
          pages cm. — (The Berenson schemes, #3)
        Summary: Wanting to get in touch with their spiritual sides, Jack's
    parents decide to move to Nepal and start a new religion, but on their way
    to Shangrilala they are separated so Jack sets out with their first disciple
    to find them, winds up at an isolated monastery, and learns some lessons
    about acceptance.
        ISBN 978–1–4677–1078–7 (trade hard cover : alk. paper)
        ISBN 978–1–4677–6189–5 (eBook)
        [1. Adventure and adventurers—Fiction. 2. Spiritual life—Fiction.
    3. Parents—Fiction. 4. Eccentrics and eccentricities—Fiction. 5. Nepal—
    Fiction. 6. Humorous stories.] I. Stevanovic, Ivica, illustrator. II. Title.
    PZ7.D6485Jabm 2015
    [Fic]—dc23   2014010782

Manufactured in the United States of America
1 – SB – 12/31/14

For all who helped along the way—family; my friends Barb, Frances, Margaret, Mary, Michelle, and Nancy; the VCFA program; and my graduate semester advisor, Martine Leavitt

CHAPTER 1

In which Jack's parents fail to pick up parenting tips

Jack let himself into the family bungalow after a long afternoon relaxing by the resort's saltwater pool. His parents were in the living room, sitting cross-legged in front of a stone Buddha. Richard Berenson rang a brass bell. Claire Berenson pressed her palms together and murmured, "Namaste."

Jack laid his towel and sunscreen on the table. "What are you doing?" he asked.

"Meditating, luv," his mom said.

"When I ring the bell," his dad said, "We empty our minds."

"Absolutely empty," his mom said.

"You're not supposed to be emptying your minds," Jack said. "You're supposed to be following Mr. and Mrs. Aiken from Ohio. I picked them out especially for you."

"Exactly what we told the manager," his dad said. "But Mr. Patel said that was an absolute no-go."

"Right after your dad hoisted me up to peek into the Aiken's bathroom window," his mom said, "Mr. Patel ran across the courtyard and shouted, 'Get away from there.'"

"You looked in the Aiken's window?"

"You bet we did," his dad said. "You said we weren't to let Todd and Carol Aiken out of our sight, that everything they did could be a key to responsible parenting."

"I said follow their *example*. I didn't mean spying on them in their own bathroom," Jack said.

"Frankly, Son," his dad said, "we wondered about that. We were able to discover that Carol Aiken dyes her hair, but we couldn't fathom what we were meant to do with that information."

"No worries, Jack," his mom said. "We've found someone far more interesting to follow around than Todd and Carol Aiken."

"That's right, Son," his dad said. "Have you met Aditi, from the great country of Nepal? She runs the yoga and meditation programs for the hotel."

"It turns out we have a knack for spirituality," his mom said.

"Shall we tell him the news?" his dad said.

"Let's."

"Oh, no. Not news," Jack muttered.

"Brace yourself, Jack," his dad said. "Since coming to Mombasa after our last setback, your mum and I have become enlightened."

"Enlightened to what?" Jack asked.

"Enlightened to our karmic destiny, that's what," his mom said. "We were running all over the world, coming up with one scheme after the next, when all along we should have been laser-focused on the great beyond."

"And here's the thrilling part," his dad said. "In honor of our enlightenment, we've invented a new religion."

"You can't just invent a religion," Jack said.

"Most people can't. But don't forget, Jack, we are the Berensons," his dad said.

"We're calling it Nosnereb. It's like Buddhism but with a Church of Englandy spin."

"Nosnereb?" Jack said. "Wait a minute, that's just—"

His dad rang the bell again and said, "Exactly."

"We didn't come here to invent a religion," Jack said. "The whole reason we came to the Namaste-For-Kids resort is so you could study other parents. Imitating top-rated parents is supposed to help your parental instincts come out. I picked the Aikens because they have two kids and have never lost them anywhere. Not even in the mall."

Jack's mom pressed her palms together and bowed her head. "The first commandment of Nosnereb is 'Forgive and forget all prior mishaps.'"

Jack folded his arms. "What are the other commandments?"

"We just have the one so far," his dad said.

"You can't expect a whole set of commandments to just spring up out of nowhere."

"Stranding me in a tree on the African plains is more than a mishap," Jack said.

Jack's mom reddened and said, "That was unfortunate. On the bright side, that very incident led us to work so hard on this new plan. We've figured out a foolproof way to make our fortune *and* not lose you again."

Jack's dad unfolded his legs and rubbed his calves. "You see, Son, spirituality is big business these days. Consumers want to know, why am I here? How did I get here? Am I coming back? Can I come back rich? So your mom and I went ahead and bought a monastery in Nepal."

"Jack, you are looking at the co-Dalai Lamas of Nosnereb," his mom said.

"That's ridiculous," Jack said. "There's no such thing as co-Dalai Lamas. Don't you think the real Dalai Lama would be mad if he heard about it?"

"That's the beauty of it," his dad said. "The Dalai Lama can't be mad—it's against his religion. And anyway, when was the last time you heard of the Dalai Lama losing a kid in a monastery?"

"Never," his mom said. "Not one documented case."

"I don't even know why you would be interested in religion," Jack said. "For one thing, you haven't been in a church since you got married. For another, you want to be rich, and I'm sure starting a religion can't be a good way to make money."

His mom snorted. "Tell that to the Vatican."

"Wait a minute," Jack said. "When you say you bought a monastery in Nepal, you don't actually mean you bought a monastery in Nepal, do you?"

"Not technically," his mom said.

Jack sat back, relieved.

"It's more of a run-down farmhouse," his mom said. "But with a little elbow grease, we'll turn it into the spectacular birthplace and worldwide headquarters of Nosnereb."

"People from all over the world will flock to Nepal to hear our teachings," his dad said. "Then those grateful pilgrims will leave us change in our donation boxes. Spare change can add up pretty quick when you don't have to pay taxes."

"Donation boxes are for the poor!" Jack said.

His mom shrugged. "We're not *not* poor."

"Son," Jack's dad said, "everybody knows, charity starts at home."

"And anyway, Jack," his mom continued, "we couldn't pass up the deal we found online. A farmhouse, with an acre of land, in the beautiful countryside of Nepal."

"Well, most of a house anyway," Jack's dad said. "You really can't expect all four walls when you're only paying $500."

"You bought a house on the internet?" Jack said. "That is the worst idea I've ever heard."

"Richard, I told you Jack would say that," his mom said.

"Jack *always* says that," his dad added.

"But this time we're way ahead of you, luv," his mom said. "You were the one that went on and on about safety. You said you were sick and tired of being lost in foreign countries."

"That's right," his dad said. "You said that

from now on, safety has to be our number one priority."

"And what could be safer than living in a monastery?" his mom asked.

"I cannot believe you got so off track," Jack said. "All I asked you to do was study Mr. and Mrs. Aiken. Now you've bought some crumbling building in a country you've never even been to?"

"Yes, but we're not allowed back in so many of the countries we *have* been to . . ."

"Get on the internet and give that house back right now," Jack said.

"Oh, we can't do that," his mom said. "We already wired the money."

In which Jack learns that Shangrilala is elusive

Jack found Aditi at the hotel's front desk. He stood on his toes and leaned over the counter. "Did you help my parents buy property in Nepal?"

The stapler in Aditi's hand clattered onto the desk and then crashed to the floor. "Certainly not," she said. "When they asked me to arrange a flight to Kathmandu, I told them Nepal didn't actually exist. That it was an idea, not a place. Perhaps not the cleverest response, but I panicked. I have relatives there, you know."

"But somehow, after following you around,

my parents have made themselves co-Dalai Lamas of an invented religion."

"Lamas? The Berensons?" Aditi snorted with laughter. "Did you hear that, Margaret?" she asked the girl manning the phones. "The Berensons and the Dalai Lama in the same sentence!"

Margaret shrieked with laughter.

"Your parents chatter through every meditation," Aditi continued. "The other guests have lodged complaints with Mr. Patel." She put her hands together, imitating Jack's mom and dad. "'Have you emptied your mind, Richard?' 'Absolutely empty, darling.' 'Look, luv, Nirvana straight ahead.'"

Jack stomped out of the reception room and called over his shoulder, "It's only funny if you're not living with them."

• • •

Jack shoved clothes into his backpack. Everything had seemed to be going so well. His eyebrows had started to grow back, and the Berensons had left the Kenyan plains for the coast. Jack had been relaxing by the pool, sipping pineapple smoothies. But while he was recovering, his parents were buying a crumbling farmhouse in Nepal.

Jack was sure Nosnereb wouldn't catch on. His mom and dad weren't even religious. Jack had gone to church with his friend Zack's family every Sunday, while Richard and Claire Berenson lounged around the living room, reading newspaper comics and doing the crossword puzzle.

Jack dug through his backpack, reaching underneath the stuffed monkey Diana had sent "gnoming" with him, now beat up after spending time with an ornery honey badger. Jack was supposed to take pictures of the monkey posing in foreign locations. But so far, gnoming had been a bust.

He fished out his notebook to update Zack on the latest catastrophe. Jack flipped through the pages. They were all blank. Where were the letters he had written while marooned on the plains? Jack had planned to mail the message to Zack and destroy the letter to Diana. Jack had decided it was too soon to ask Diana if she wanted to be his girlfriend. Or too risky. It was too . . . something.

His parents must have taken the letters. On top of everything else, now they were reading his mail. Had they picked that up from the Aikens? Jack had interviewed the Aiken children for three hours, and none of them had said anything about their parents nosing around in personal notebooks.

Jack charged into the bungalow's living room. His mom and dad were pressing their palms together, bowing, and whispering, "Namaste. Nosnereb."

"Did you take the letters from my notebook?" Jack said.

"Yes, we did," his dad said.

"You have no right to read my personal stuff," Jack said. "It's private."

"We didn't read them, you goose," his mom said. "We mailed them."

"Mailed them! Both of them?"

"Now don't thank us, Son," his dad said. "We were happy to do it."

"You see, Jack," his mom said, "thanks to your mature and rational influence, your dad and I are getting more organized by the minute. No more procrastination for us."

"We are done with putting things off and hoping somebody else gets around to it," his dad said.

"But I didn't want to send those letters," Jack cried. "Well, not both of them."

Jack's parents glanced at each other. "We didn't see that coming," his dad said.

"Wait a minute," Jack said. "How did you even get Diana's address?"

"We didn't," his mom said. "We sent everything to Zack with a note asking him to pass along Diana's letter."

It would have been bad enough for Diana to get that letter. Now Zack would read it first?

"I suppose it's lucky we're going to Nepal," Jack said. "I won't be able to show my face in Pennsylvania until everyone I know has left for college."

"You're very welcome," his mom said.

"Namaste," his dad said.

Jack peered out the window as the plane began its descent. Mountains covered with green forests stretched out below him. Small houses began to appear, perched atop cleared plateaus. Jack wondered if one of them was the farmhouse his parents had bought on the internet. He squinted to see if he could spot a missing wall, but the plane was too high. They dropped in altitude and approached Kathmandu until the plane landed with a thud at Tribhuvan International Airport.

At the immigration checkpoint, Jack's parents told a Nepali official that the family had come to climb Mt. Everest. The official asked if they had filed for the required permit.

"Permit?" Jack's dad asked, glancing at his mom.

"Ah," his mom said. "What we meant was we will *not* climb Mt. Everest. We are firmly against it, so don't try to talk us into it. We'll only climb a mountain that *doesn't* need a permit."

"A smaller one," Jack's dad added. "More of a hill than a mountain."

His mom nodded. "Probably just a slope."

The official flipped through the passports, eyeing the deportation stamps.

"Many unfortunate misunderstandings, Namaste," Jack's mom said.

Jack noticed his parents didn't mention anything about being co-Dalai Lamas.

The Berensons stepped out the doors of the airport and were engulfed by a crowd of shouting men. Jack thought his family had stumbled into some sort of riot until his dad collared one of the men and shouted, "You!" The man he'd grabbed led them to a taxi.

His mom directed the driver to the Thamel section of Kathmandu. She leaned over to Jack and said, "That's where all the backpackers hang out."

Jack sighed. Was there no place on the planet these backpackers weren't hanging around? They were like the common cold of the traveling public. No matter where a person went, there they were.

* * *

The streets of Thamel were choked with taxis, motorcycles, pedestrians, and rickshaws. Women in saris weaved around westerners in baseball caps. The driver barreled down the narrow cobblestone streets, leaning on his horn when somebody got in his way and sometimes when nobody got in his way.

Narrow shops overflowed with wooden masks, statues, DVDs, trekking gear, bins of loose tea, bright scarves, and heavy wool sweaters. An old man crouched by the side of the road, playing an instrument that sounded like a fiddle. Signs were painted on every available wall. From what Jack could gather, a visitor was meant to change money, rent a room, see a travel agent, and climb a mountain.

The taxi dropped them off at the Total-Peace-Out Guesthouse. Jack stumbled through the incense-filled lobby and found a clerk lounging with his feet up on a rickety desk. The man, an American wearing a tie-dye T-shirt and some kind of skirt, had looked up and said, "Peace Out."

"Uh, thanks. You too," Jack said. "Do you

have any rooms?"

Jack was disappointed to learn that the Total-Peace-Out Guesthouse *did* have rooms available. He spent the evening putting out incense sticks when nobody was looking and fell asleep with a pillow over his head to filter out some of the smoke.

● ● ●

The next morning Jack and his parents hauled their backpacks through the crowded streets of Kathmandu.

"We have learned our lesson about renting Jeeps," his mom said over her shoulder. "I said to your dad, no more zooming away in a Jeep without Jack."

"Good-bye to that," his dad said.

"This time, we're traveling by bus," his mom said.

His dad nodded. "Leave the driving to somebody else is what we said."

"We just hop off at Shangrilala," his mom said, "and then we are ready to buckle down and get to work."

"Are you sure that's a real town?" Jack said. "It sounds made up."

"Of course it's real, Jack," his mom said. "The people who sold us the farmhouse certainly know the name of their own town."

"Okay, but don't we have to pick up the keys somewhere? Is the real estate office in Shangrilala too?" Jack asked.

"Well, Son," his dad said, "there's no point in locking the front door when a whole side of the house is missing."

Jack supposed that was true.

Jack's parents had a long conversation with the ticket agent at the bus station. He had never heard of Shangrilala. The man asked Jack's mom and dad what it was near. They didn't know. The ticket agent told them that since he was from east of Kathmandu, Shangrilala must be west. Jack did not think those were very detailed directions.

The bus careened down a narrow highway, hemmed in by another bus in front and a large truck nipping at its back wheels. Vehicles of all

shapes and sizes whooshed by from the opposite direction. Sheets of gray rock rose up the left side of the road. The right side dropped steeply away below its stone guardrails. At the bottom of the valley, a narrow river twisted along with the road.

Six hours later, the Berensons still hadn't found Shangrilala. Jack's parents had asked for directions from everyone that spoke English, but nobody had heard of it.

The bus barreled by houses perched on the edges of steep slopes. Jack thought some of them looked like they would need a helicopter to get in and out of. He could imagine the neighbors' conversations:

"Have you seen our son?"

"Possibly. A kid wearing a yellow T-shirt rolled to the bottom of the ravine about an hour ago."

The bus swerved to avoid an oncoming truck that had drifted into its lane. Jack wondered if he'd be better off not looking at the road. His fingers had turned white from gripping the armrest.

"Richard," his mom said. "We have a captive audience on this bus, and here we are, lollygagging about, admiring the scenery."

"Just so," his dad said. "If we pick up some disciples now, they can help build that fourth wall we're going to need."

Jack's mom got up from her seat.

"Wait," Jack said. "What are you doing?"

"Launching Nosnereb," his mom said.

Jack's parents staggered to the front of the bus. Bracing her leg against the back of the driver's seat, his mom turned to face the passengers. She pressed her palms together and said, "Namaste, fellow seekers of truth and knowledge."

Jack sank lower in his seat.

"I'm Claire Berenson," his mom said. "This is my husband, Richard. And there's our son, Jack. Right there, the one slumped in his seat."

The couple across the aisle stared at Jack. He waved.

"We have rather exciting news," his mom continued. "You are the first to hear about a groundbreaking new religion called Nosnereb."

"Nosnereb," his dad repeated, clutching at a seat top.

"Nosnereb," his mom said, "combines the most popular elements of Buddhism, like bells and flags, with the down-to-earth pragmatism of the Church of England."

"Henry the VIII was nothing if not pragmatic," his dad said. "You don't unload that many wives by being a dreamer."

A young man with a heap of dark red hair sat in the row in front of Jack. He leaned forward and said, "Cool. This could be it."

Jack's mom explained that reincarnation would be available in Nosnereb, but only if a person felt like it. Also, a person could decide the particulars of the reincarnation, so everybody could come back rich. Nosnereb didn't have any relics yet, so Nosnerebists were encouraged to donate silver chalices and old-looking shrouds. They were still working on a logo; so far it looked sort of like the Nike swoosh. And since Nosnereb was a blend of church and temple, Nosnerebists would worship in a chemple.

The redhead in front of Jack said, "Chemple? That is awesome."

"The chemple," Jack's mom continued, "will be located in the beautiful village of Shangrilala."

"By the by," his dad said, "does anyone know where we can find Shangrilala?"

Jack looked around the bus. Either nobody knew how to get there or they weren't telling.

"No worries, we'll track it down eventually," his mom said. "In any case—the moment we decided to invent our own spiritual movement, I looked at Richard and said, 'You know what we need?'"

A particularly sharp curve in the road threw Jack's dad to the floor. He staggered up and said, "Disciples."

The young man with the wild red hair jumped to his feet. "I'm in, dude!"

Jack's dad gave the man a thumbs-up. His mom said, "Who else is in? Who else?"

Nobody else was in.

● ● ●

An hour later, the bus veered into a gravel parking lot.

Jack had already been introduced to his parent's first disciple—Harry from Connecticut. Harry was eighteen and on a trip around the world to find himself. So far, Harry had looked in Thailand and India with no luck. Now he was looking in Nepal.

The other passengers on the bus filed out, collected their luggage, and set off on a dusty path down the mountainside. The bus driver stood in the aisle, staring at Jack's parents.

Jack's mom said, "Sir, how long will we be at this stop?"

"I go no further," the driver answered.

"Ah," Jack's dad said. "Then when can we expect the bus that carries us on from here?"

"Three days. The road closes for strike tomorrow. You must get off the bus."

CHAPTER 3

In which Jack exits a vehicle in an original fashion

"Three days!" Jack said to the driver. "Sir, do you know where Shangrilala is located and how we could get there from here? Can we call a taxi? Can we rent a car? And if we really can't go anywhere for three days, where is the closest hotel?"

The man wrinkled his forehead. "You must leave the bus."

The driver hurried them down the steps and threw their backpacks off the roof rack. He locked the bus door and set off on the dirt path.

"No worries," Jack's mom said. "I feel we must be getting very close to Shangrilala. We hardly require a bus to complete our journey. We'll just wait for a car to come along."

"Do you mean hitchhiking?" Jack said. "Everybody knows that's dangerous. We could get picked up by robbers. Or even serial killers."

"Now, Jack," his mom said, "who ever heard of a Nepali serial killer?"

"They could call him the Everest Evil Guy," Harry said. "But seriously, you can't be too careful about Yetis. How many footprints are we gonna find before people wake up and see the truth?" He shrugged. "But they don't drive, so that's cool."

Jack's dad snorted. "Yetis. Good one, Harry."

"Even if hitchhiking was a good idea, which it isn't," Jack said, "what would we hitchhike on? There aren't any cars. It'll be dark soon, and then what will we do? We don't even have tents."

"What we will do is," his dad said, looking around at the empty parking lot, "well, we simply will—"

"We should probably try to catch up to all those other people that went down the dirt path," Jack said. "Maybe we can stay in their village."

"Look, Richard," his mom said, "a truck just swerved around the bend."

Harry slapped Jack on the back. "Have a little more faith, my fellow Nosnerebist."

Jack watched the truck as it barreled toward them. It looked like a big dump truck, the kind that was used on construction sites.

"It's not even going the right way," Jack said.

His mom whipped the scarf from around her neck and waved it over her head. The truck slammed on its brakes, skidded past them, and backed up.

"Namaste," his dad said to the two men in the cab. "May we hitch a lift from you fine fellows? We're just on our way to Shangrilala. We realize you'd have to turn around, but we're willing to pay you for any inconvenience."

The two men put their heads together and spoke in rapid Nepalese.

Jack looked at the truck. Slabs of what looked like quartz or marble were piled high on the truck bed. He doubted that would be very comfortable to sit on.

One of the men said, "The place you are going is this way," pointing in the direction the bus had just come from. "To go there, it is 20,000 rupees for all."

"That's $200!" Jack said.

Harry rifled through his day pack. "Let me see what I got. Now that I'm the first disciple of Nosnereb, I should probably take a vow of poverty anyway."

The driver revved the engine and said, "We must go quickly to be off the road by sunrise. The strike starts at dawn."

Jack's dad ignored the driver's impatience. "I should warn you, sirs," he said, "I'm a bit of a cutthroat negotiator. I will consult with my banker. Then you may prepare yourselves for my first salvo." His dad leaned down to Jack and whispered, "How much do we have?"

The traveler's checks had been entrusted to Jack, as he had been voted least likely to lose them. "Eight hundred dollars. But, Dad, two hundred is too much to pay for a ride."

"I'll handle this, Son," his dad said. He turned to the driver. "We will give you $200 for the fare, on the condition that our two younger travelers get to sit up front in the cab."

His dad winked at Jack and whispered, "Placing the children *inside* the vehicle sounds distinctly like careful parenting, don't you think?"

The man driving the vehicle shook his head no and then pointed at Jack. "Only the small one," he said.

"I'm not that small," Jack said.

Jack's dad folded his arms. "I'll meet you halfway," he said to the driver. "Agreed."

His dad turned to his mom. "Claire, getting thrown off that bus was a real stroke of luck. We've finally found people who actually know how to get us to Shangrilala."

His mom nodded. "We must have driven right by it."

Jack's dad handed over the money. He and Jack's mom hoisted themselves onto the back of the truck. Harry threw their packs up and climbed in after them. The man on the passenger side of the vehicle moved over. Jack wedged in next to him.

The driver threw the truck in gear, and the vehicle lurched forward. Despite the twists and turns, the truck rolled down the narrow road at breakneck speed. Jack put his arms through the straps of his backpack so the pack rested on his stomach before securing the waistband clip. He looked like a pregnant lady, but if the driver got into an accident, the backpack could be a makeshift airbag. Hopefully, it would cushion him as he flew through the windshield.

The sun set over the mountains. The truck barreled past the occasional headlights of other vehicles racing to their destinations before the start of the strike. The driver had put on headphones, but Jack could hear the music he blasted from the other side of the cab. The man next to him pulled a flask from his pocket, drained it, and promptly fell asleep.

Jack turned his head and peered through the glass at the back of the truck. He could barely make out the lumps of his mom, his dad, and Harry, lying on the slabs of stone with their

jackets drawn over their heads. He snuggled down in his seat and tried to get comfortable. It could be worse. He could be outside.

As the hours rolled by, Jack drifted in and out of sleep. The truck rounded a sharp curve, and the man in the middle seat slammed into him, pushing him against the door. Through Jack's sleepy haze, he heard a faint click.

His door flew open.

Jack flailed, trying to grasp something. His hands found only air. He hit the ground on top

of his backpack and rolled over lumps of grass.

Jack struggled to his feet in time to see the taillights swing around a curve and the passenger door close shut.

Jack felt around his body for injuries. His backpack had mostly protected him. As far as he could tell, he would end up with some bruises and scrapes, but nothing was broken.

Jack held out his hand in the moonless night and waved it in front of his face. Now that the lights from the truck were gone, he couldn't see it. The road was a few yards in front of him. A low wall bordered the opposite side. Beyond the wall, a canyon plummeted hundreds of feet toward a winding river. Jack decided he'd better not make a move until he could tell where he was going. He could imagine thinking he was headed the right way, tripping over the wall, and plummeting down the cliff.

Jack slid the backpack off his stomach and put it on his back. He might not be able to see anything, but a vehicle could come along any minute. He had to be ready to run to the road and flag it down. The truck he'd fallen out of might have turned around already. Sooner or later that driver would take his headphones off, look around, and notice he was down a man.

But what if the driver had noticed already and decided not to mention it? The man had seemed pretty determined to get to where he was going before the strike started. Maybe he wouldn't want to lose time by racing back for Jack.

Jack reminded himself that he always thought of the worst possible scenarios. That was how his brain worked, and it was up to him to control it. After all, what had really happened? He had just fallen out of a truck. Somebody, somewhere in the world, probably fell out of a truck every day. He didn't have any serious injuries. He was just standing by the side of the road. Slightly bruised. Waiting for a ride.

Minutes ticked by, then what seemed like hours. There were no vehicles coming or going. Jack sat down and hugged his knees, shivering through the cool night and listening for the rumble of a vehicle motor. Each time his mind considered how his situation could keep getting worse, he reminded himself to relax.

Finally, the sky lightened to a gray dawn.

At least now Jack could see where he was going. If he started walking, he was bound to find some help. He strained his ears to listen for cars or trucks as he stumbled down the road.

Jack walked for half an hour. He came around a bend, hoping to see a village or even a lone house. There was nothing but more tarmac, twisting along the mountainside.

A hundred yards ahead, Jack spotted a bundle of old clothes on the embankment. As he got closer, he realized the pile of clothes had red hair.

"Harry," Jack called, jogging toward the heap. "Harry, is that you?"

The heap sat up. It was Harry.

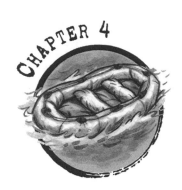

CHAPTER 4

In which Jack considers transportation options

"Dude," Harry said, "what are you doing here? Where's the truck?"

"The door opened and I fell out," Jack answered. "What happened to you?"

"Your dad rolled over in the middle of the night and pushed me over the side."

"Oh, no. Are you hurt?"

"Just bruised," Harry said. "You?"

"Same. I don't suppose my dad woke up and noticed."

"Not that I saw, but it all happened really really fast."

They stood in silence for a moment. Then Harry said, "I was thinking this might be a test. You know, to see if I'm worthy of being a Nosnerebist."

"It's not a test," Jack said.

"But maybe you saying it's not a test is *part* of the test."

Jack didn't answer. If Harry thought he was in the middle of a spiritual test, that was Harry's business.

"Guess all we can do is start walking," Harry said. "We'll catch up to your parents eventually."

Jack and Harry walked for an hour without seeing any cars. They rounded a bend and spotted a cement building on the ravine side of the road. The place had a faded Coca-Cola bottle painted on its side. A haphazard pile of bricks held its tin roof in place.

"Finally," Jack said.

"Civilization, here we come," Harry added.

They jogged the rest of the way down the road and ducked into the entrance. A middle-aged woman sat at the counter, working on a piece of embroidery and humming to the radio.

Jack asked the woman for a phone. She laid her embroidery down, went to the refrigerator, and came back with two Cokes.

Jack took the sodas and handed one to Harry. "I don't think she understands me," he said.

"It's all good," Harry said, using a bottle opener to pop the cap off his soda, "We'll just chill here until your mom and dad come back."

"Harry," Jack said, "I'm sorry to tell you that my parents could have gotten pretty far before they noticed either one of us was missing. But that's not the really bad news. Once they notice, they'll come up with a *rescue plan*. The rescue plan will probably be something like, 'Why don't we paraglide over the mountains until we find them?'"

"Nah. Really?"

"Very really."

Harry looked like he might not hold up against this alarming news. Jack reminded himself that while he was used to being lost, it was all brand new to Harry from Connecticut.

"Paraglide over the mountains to find us?" Harry said. "That wouldn't make any sense at all."

"I'm not saying they will definitely paraglide. I'm just saying they might. "

"Then . . . but what about Nosnereb? I was counting on being the first and foremost disciple. Maybe even end up as a bishop or a cardinal or something. Your mom and dad seemed so confident. I figured it was gonna be a huge hit."

"Well," Jack said, considering a way to break things gently, "Nosnereb is a very new religion. My parents made it up about a week ago."

"I get that it's new," Harry said. "That's what's so cool about it. But what do you mean, they made it up? Didn't they get a sign? Like a burning bush or something?"

"Uh," Jack said, "no burning bush that I'm aware of."

"But if they didn't get some kind of sign, how did they know all that stuff about it? How did they even know what to call it?"

"*Nosnereb* is *Berenson* spelled backwards," Jack said.

Harry stared at him.

"It's okay, Harry," Jack said. "Trust me, things could be way worse. It's not like we're stranded in the middle of nowhere. We'll track down my mom and dad. Once we find them, you can grill them about this new religion. I know my mom said a lot of stuff on the bus, but I'm pretty sure she was just making it up as she went along."

Harry had the same expression that Zack's dog did when it wolfed down its dinner and then realized the food was gone: a mix of regret and despair.

"But you never know," Jack said, hoping to soften the blow. "I could be wrong."

Harry ran a hand through his wild hair and muttered, "I can't believe how hard it is to find myself. Seems like it should be easier than this."

Jack tried talking to the woman again, this time using his hands as a kind of international sign language. She didn't seem to understand that rocking a pretend baby was supposed to mean Jack was somebody's son or that when Jack cupped his hands around his eyes and looked in all directions, he meant he was lost.

Harry hadn't helped by shouting, "Baby!" and "You're searching for something!"

The woman motioned for Jack and Harry to wait in the shop. After a half hour, she brought back a man named Mr. Shrestha, who spoke English. At the end of a long conversation, Jack said, "I realize there's a strike, but there must be some kind of transportation."

"None," Mr. Shrestha said, "Unless . . ."

"Unless what?" Jack asked.

Mr. Shrestha turned away from Jack and spoke softly to himself. "No, I cannot. And yet, I must consider others. I should not be selfish."

Jack tapped him on the shoulder. "Mr. Shrestha?"

Mr. Shrestha turned and said, "Yes! As I was saying, *unless* you buy my raft and use the river to catch up with your relatives. No one's striking on the river. Though I would be truly heartbroken to sell my most prized possession."

"Oh," Jack said, "well I wouldn't want to break your—"

"But I would get over it," Mr. Shrestha said.

"Dude," Harry said to Jack. "We don't even have sleeping bags."

Mr. Shrestha nodded and said to Jack, "Your demon-haired friend is very shrewd."

Harry did have a point, Jack thought. Even if his parents were about to do something sensible, like drive back to where they had last seen him instead of paragliding around the mountains, they wouldn't be able to do it for three days. But as Mr. Shrestha pointed out, there was no way to close down the river. And anyway, Jack had already seen the river enough times out of the bus window. It was narrow; it just looked like a big stream.

"I guess nothing could go too wrong on a raft," Jack said. "If you really wanted to sell it."

"I must sacrifice my own wishes to help my fellow man," Mr. Shrestha said.

"Do you know how far it is to Shangrilala?" Jack asked.

Mr. Shrestha said, "Shangrilala? Oh, not far.

You'll get there quick on a raft."

Jack sighed. They must have gone past Shangrilala shortly after leaving Kathmandu. They had been driving farther away from it ever since. "How will we know when we get to the town?"

"Uh . . ." Mr. Shrestha said, "I believe there is a sign."

"All right, we'll take it," Jack said.

"You are very fortunate to get this bargain," Mr. Shrestha said. "I sell it to you for only 500,000 rupees."

"That's $5,000!" Jack said. "We don't have $5,000."

"Okay, okay," Mr. Shrestha said, waving his arms. "Since you are my friend, I will give you a discount."

"How much of a discount?" Jack asked.

"How much do you have?" Mr. Shrestha asked.

Harry said, "I got nothing. My backpack is on the truck."

Jack thumbed through his mom and dad's traveler's checks. "I have $600. But I can't give you all of that because we need to buy supplies. It's not even my money. It's my mom and dad's, and for all I know, this might be their lifesavings."

Mr. Shrestha narrowed his eyes. "I see you are a hard bargainer. I tell you what: I will give you this raft almost free. Only $300." Mr. Shrestha looked into the distance with a pained expression. "I will even give you the bag of equipment that came with it. I cannot go any cheaper without starving my own children."

Jack thought the price was still too high, but he did not want to be involved in starving any children. "Okay," he said, "sold."

* * *

While they waited for Mr. Shrestha to bring the raft, Harry said, "Jack, you don't look freaked out. If I was your age and I fell out of a truck in a foreign country and had no idea where my parents were, I'd be like, 'What? Seriously?'"

"I'm more like, 'What? Seriously? *Again*?'" Jack said. "Harry, I've spent extended periods of time fending for myself in the wilderness.

So, while I didn't see this coming, I probably should have."

Harry stared at him. "Dude."

Yes, Jack thought. Dude, indeed.

● ● ●

As Mr. Shrestha worked the foot pump to inflate the raft, Jack began to have second thoughts. There were more patches along the rubber than he would have expected. "Sir," Jack said, "are you sure the raft is in good working order? It looks like it's been repaired. A lot."

"That's why I got it so cheap," Mr. Shrestha said.

Jack pressed his lips together. He was sure he had not gotten a good deal on the raft. "Oh," Jack said to Mr. Shrestha. "But you've used it?"

"One time."

"Only once? But then, why did you buy it?" Jack asked.

"I see tourists on the river and say to myself, 'Shrestha, that's a good business.' So I invest in a secondhand raft and take tourists on a day trip. The longest six hours of my life. 'What kind of bird is that, Mr. Shrestha?' I say, 'A small bird.' 'Where is the toilet, Mr. Shrestha?' I say, 'There is no toilet.' 'Mr. Shrestha, did I mention I am lactose intolerant?' I say, 'Yes, many times.' 'Mr. Shrestha, what is the dairy-free option for lunch?' I say, 'Do not worry about your intolerance, I did not bring food.' 'Do you like Americans, Mr. Shrestha?' I say, 'Not so far.' 'Look at these pictures of my children, Mr. Shrestha. Their names are Joshua and Emily. They're lactose intolerant too. Aren't they adorable?' I say, 'I want to cry.'

"It took me many days of silence to recover. Why do you Americans fly halfway across the world to sit in a boat and talk about lactose?"

"I don't know," Jack said.

"Rafting is for the experience," Harry said. "You know, wind in your hair, close to nature. All that."

Mr. Shrestha seemed to take a dim view of wind in anybody's hair. "You see what I am talking about?" he said to Jack. "I don't have time to float around in nature. I am too busy trying to keep nature out of my house."

● ● ●

Jack walked over to the ridge and peered down at the river. The water seemed to gently amble along.

Harry came up behind him. "We got to look at this as an adventure. I'll start loading supplies on the counter. Good news: they got a lot of titaura in there."

"A lot of what?" Jack asked.

"Titaura. It's awesome candy. When I get home, I'm gonna write my congressman and find out why we don't have it in Connecticut. If he tells me it's some kind of trade embargo, I'm gonna say, 'Dude, you have just lost my vote.'"

Jack wasn't convinced that candy could ruin the political aspirations of a congressman, no matter how good it was. "All right, Harry, but don't only buy empty calories. We'll need real nutrition to sustain us on the river."

Harry slapped Jack on the back. "You sound like my grandma. Lighten up."

Lighten up? Jack had been flung out of a truck while hitchhiking in a remote region of

Nepal, which put his parent's record at 0–3. But Harry thought Jack should lighten up.

Jack didn't know what kind of fairy-tale life Harry from Connecticut had been living, but Harry was about to experience the Berenson lifestyle.

Jack rifled through the raft's equipment bag. It contained two oars; two life jackets; a mess kit with two tin plates, a pot, and utensils; and a worn-out plastic tarp.

Two white helmets with chin straps rolled around the bottom of the bag.

Jack followed Harry into the store. Harry piled small plastic bags packed with a gel-like substance on the counter and muttered, "Just got to be careful not to get the spicy ones."

Jack surveyed the supply options. Considering the choices he was usually left with, the cramped store was packed with valuable resources. Jack collected five boxes of wooden matches. He grabbed a selection of waterproof plastic bags. He examined the food shelf and grabbed four chicken-flavored noodle packets called Wai Wai and a couple of liter bottles of water.

He paused at a display of disposable cameras. Jack had promised Diana he would take the stuffed monkey she had given him "gnoming." But instead of posing the monkey at various foreign locations, Jack had let the stuffed animal get mauled by a wild animal in Kenya. He only had one hand-drawn picture of it: the monkey swinging from an acacia tree.

Jack grabbed one of the cameras.

Jack and Harry put the supplies and Jack's backpack in plastic bags and tied the bags to the rope that encircled the top of the raft. He and Harry struggled down the footpath to the river, carrying the raft between them. Mr. Shrestha trailed behind them.

At water's edge, Jack and Harry scrambled into the raft and grabbed the oars. Mr. Shrestha pushed them off, launching them into the river. As they rounded the first bend, Mr. Shrestha called after them. "Just don't take the—!"

"What did he say?" Harry asked.

"I don't know. Don't take the something."

"Should we go back and ask?"

"The current's pulling us downstream pretty fast," Jack said. "We'd have to beach the raft and walk back."

"Seems like if it was important, he would've told us before we were floating away."

"Seems like it," Jack said.

CHAPTER 5

In which Jack takes the river less traveled

Jack and Harry drifted downstream. Jack found that if he angled his oar correctly in the water, he could steer the boat toward the middle of the river. Steep cliffs rose up on either side of them; millions of years of water had cut a course through the stone. The road at the top of the cliffs had disappeared. Jack couldn't see if it was still above them or not.

The sun warmed Jack's skin. He ran his fingers in the water. It smelled clean and felt cool on his fingertips.

Jack had wondered if rafting required any

special skills, but now that he was actually on the raft, he realized it wasn't complicated at all. He could see why tourists would want to take in the scenery while relaxing on the river. And anyway, Jack figured that traveling with Harry on a raft was safer than traveling with his parents on anything.

As the day wore on, Jack scouted likely places to camp. He spotted a long white beach.

"What about stopping there, Harry?" Jack asked.

Harry nodded, and they steered the boat toward the shore. It landed on the powdery white sand with a soft, scraping sound.

They pulled the raft up on the beach. Jack rolled the tarp out on the sand. Harry went to find firewood, while Jack dug a fire pit and got out the mess kit.

Harry came back from scouting along the bank, his arms full of dried-out branches. As the sun passed over the mountains, Jack lit the kindling. The fire cast a cheery glow on the beach. Jack held the pot of water over the flames to boil the Wai Wai noodles. He carefully portioned the noodles out onto the two tin plates.

"Harry," Jack said, "besides trying to find yourself, what made you decide to travel all over the world? Do you come from a traveling family?"

"Sort of," Harry answered. "My parents only go to resorts in the Caribbean. The kind where you sit on the beach and drink out of a coconut. But my grandparents used to take trips all over the world. I must've picked up the travel bug from them." Harry added softly, "Only, they don't leave Connecticut anymore. They had a bad experience."

"Oh, no," Jack said. "What happened to them?"

"It was pretty epic. They went on a safari, which they had done like a million times before, but on that last one, they got left behind in the wilderness. Roving troops of baboons took everything they had. Even my grandma's glasses."

Jack choked on his noodles.

Harry slapped Jack on the back and said, "My gram says if she ever gets her hands on the

Berensteins, they'll wish they'd never set eyes on Agnes Grady."

Jack coughed and cleared his airway. "That's awful."

"Cheer up, Jack," Harry said. "It's not like *you* left my grandparents in the African wilderness."

● ● ●

The stars came out, bright white against the inky-blue sky. Jack and Harry had loaded the mess kit back on the raft so they could get an early start in the morning. They lay on the tarp, chewing on titaura. The first bag was fruity, and Jack liked it so much Harry got another bag off the raft. That one set Jack's mouth on fire. Harry looked at the package and said, "No way. There's a picture of a chili right there."

Jack told Harry that he wasn't sure if Diana was his girlfriend and showed him the patched-up stuffed monkey. Harry held the monkey up to the firelight and said, "I don't know if she's your girlfriend, but you are definitely her boyfriend. Nobody but a boyfriend would put up with dragging that thing around."

Jack sat the monkey on the tarp and took a picture of it. The flash burst like a lone firework. Jack explained how his parents had mailed Diana a letter he wrote but had not meant to actually send, asking if she wanted to be his girlfriend.

Harry nodded sagely, as if stories of parents embarrassing kids were as old as time. He explained to Jack that he'd decided to travel the world after viewing his parents' day-to-day lives. His parents were corporate trainers and ran weekend seminars. They were paid to take executive lambs and bring back executive lions, but mostly they just brought back executive lambs that had been to a weekend seminar. Harry had decided there was more to life than that.

"When I decided to go find myself, I had no idea how hard it was gonna be," Harry said.

"How did you even figure out you needed to find yourself? What tipped you off?" Jack asked.

"There I was, growing up in this small town," Harry said, "going to prep school with all these tennis-playing dudes in madras shorts, and I'm like, this ain't me. I don't know who is me, but this ain't it."

Jack thought the state education authorities should have a word with the teachers at that prep school. Somebody there was allowing students to say "ain't." "How will you know when you've done it? When you're finally found?"

Harry groaned. "I don't know. I thought it would be this big lightning bolt. You know, get out of Connecticut and see the world and I'd just see something and go, 'Whoa, that's me.' A couple times I thought I was onto something. Like in India, I thought I could be a mahout and have my own elephant."

"That sounds like it would be a very interesting career," Jack said. "If you like elephants."

"Yeah, except I found out it takes years of training. In Thailand, I thought about becoming a scuba instructor. That looked totally cool. All the instructors were hangin' out on the beach like rock stars."

"Are you fascinated by fish, Harry?"

"Not as much as I thought I'd be. And then yesterday, I was gonna be a Nosnereb disciple.

You know, get in on the ground floor of a religion. That has to be cool. But here I am, the same Harry, no direction whatsoever."

"But, Harry," Jack said, "why do you have to travel all over the world looking for yourself? Why don't you just do what you're naturally good at?"

"There's the problem, dude," Harry said. "I can't figure that out."

• • •

As the dawn broke, Jack rolled over on his side. A long, gray leather bag lay a few feet away from the tarp. Jack didn't remember that bag.

He sat up and stared at it.

The bag stared back at Jack and blinked.

"Harry!" Jack whispered, shaking Harry's shoulder. "Harry! Get up!"

Harry groaned and rolled over. "Dude, it's zero-dark thirty."

Jack scrambled to his feet. He pulled Harry into a sitting position and pointed.

Harry whispered, "What is . . . is that a—"

"Crocodile," Jack answered.

Harry stumbled to his feet. "If there's one, there might be more."

They backed toward the raft.

The crocodile inched forward on the beach. Its eyes were hooded, as if the animal was sleepy, but it kept a close watch as they edged toward the boat.

Jack and Harry jumped on the raft. "We'll have to leave the tarp behind," Jack said.

He grabbed an oar. Mack the monkey caught his eye. The stuffed animal was hanging from a tree branch. "Harry," Jack said, "I just have to get that monkey before we go."

"Dude, leave it. You could get yourself killed over a stuffed animal."

That was true. Jack had learned that lesson in Kenya. But he couldn't imagine arriving home without the monkey. What was he supposed to say? "So . . . I left your gift hanging from a tree in Nepal." Diana would think he was a loser.

"I'll just knock it down with the oar," Jack said, stretching his arm out from inside the raft.

The monkey's Velcro paws were looped around a branch. Jack kept one eye on the crocodile while he pushed the end of the oar through the monkey's arms. He yanked the monkey down, and it fell to the ground.

The crocodile swung its massive head in the direction of the movement. It lunged at the monkey, and its powerful jaws snapped shut over the stuffed animal's face.

"No," Jack yelled. "Give that back right now!" He hit the crocodile over the head with the oar. The crocodile turned toward the raft. It flung the monkey away and charged.

Jack slid the oar under the monkey and scooped it up off the sand. "Push off, Harry," he said. "Push off now!"

Harry dug his oar into the sand and pushed the raft into the river. Jack slowly pulled in the oar, balancing the monkey on the flat side of the paddle. Once the raft had floated toward the middle of the river, Jack looked back at the beach.

The tip of the crocodile's tail disappeared underwater.

"Where did it go?" Jack said, peering over the side of the raft.

"I don't know," Harry said, "but let's not wait to find out."

Jack felt a bump underneath his feet. "It's under the raft," he said.

Jack dug his oar into the water. Harry was on the other side of the raft, his eyes wide, stabbing at the river. They turned the boat downstream.

Jack heard a splash. The opposite bank of the river had filled with crocodiles. Some were longer than the boat. One by one, they slipped into the water.

"Harry," Jack said. "You were right. There is more than one."

"Where?"

Jack looked back at the bank. "Um, I think they're all underwater now," he said.

Jack scanned the river's sandy bottom. The crocodiles moved toward the raft like a fleet of reptile submarines.

A crocodile surfaced near the boat. Jack whacked it with his oar and yelled, "Paddle, Harry! Paddle as fast as you can!" He pushed his oar in the water with deep, long strokes.

"What could go wrong on a raft?" Harry

cried. "Crocodiles are a pretty epic way to go wrong!"

Jack hit another crocodile over the head.

They paddled downriver, the crocodiles following them, until the banks narrowed and the water funneled into small, choppy rapids. Jack didn't know if that was good news or bad news. He couldn't see the crocodiles anymore. He only hoped the reptiles had turned back to their cove to wait for more hapless humans.

Jack and Harry paddled for an hour. The sandy banks disappeared. The river had narrowed, and steep cliffs hemmed it in. Jack and Harry drifted with the current, panting and sweating.

Crocodiles, Jack thought. The last thing Jack had expected was crocodiles. Why hadn't Mr. Shrestha mentioned the man-eaters? He and Harry had been lounging on the sand all night, while prehistoric killers had been lurching around in the darkness.

"Sorry about yelling at you," Harry said. "I'm not used to this stuff. The last thing you're gonna find in Connecticut is a crocodile."

"That's all right, Harry," Jack said. "You should have heard me the first time *I* thought I was about to die. If I had been with somebody, I don't know what they would have thought."

As they floated down the river, Harry went on croc watch while Jack steered the raft away from rocks. Drifting along in the middle of the river, Jack put the oar down and picked up the monkey. The crocodile had taken out one of its eyes. The other eye looked bad enough; duct tape from Jack's last repair job held it in place.

Jack ripped off the bottom of his T-shirt and fashioned an eye patch for the empty eye socket. The animal looked like a deranged monkey-pirate. Maybe when he got home, Jack could take it to some kind of stuffed animal repair shop.

Harry glanced at the monkey. "Does your girl have a sense of humor?"

Jack didn't answer. He wasn't actually sure. Diana laughed at some of his jokes, but other times—like when she had spilled ketchup all over her white jeans and Jack said, "Now they're tie-dye!"—she didn't think Jack was funny at all. Jack supposed he'd find out how lighthearted

Diana really was when she got her first look at what used to be Mack the monkey.

* * *

At midmorning, Jack looked down the river and said, "Harry, we better pull over." The river split into two waterways, one veering right and the other veering left. Jack and Harry paddled the raft over to a pile of boulders.

"How are we supposed to know which way to go?" Harry asked.

Jack stared at the fork in the river. "I wonder if this was what Mr. Shrestha meant when he yelled, 'Just don't take the' something. Hmm. I'm sure we need to stay to the right. The left side veers farther away from the road."

Harry nodded. "I will bow to your superior experience in the wilderness."

They paddled to the right.

CHAPTER 6

In which Jack proposes a trade

Throughout the rest of the day, Jack and Harry took turns paddling and scouting for crocodiles. On either side of them, rocky shoals rose up into steep granite cliffs. Jack hoped the change in terrain meant that they were out of crocodile territory. When he had bought the raft, he'd only worried about the patches holding up. Now he had to consider that he and Harry only had a piece of rubber between them and known killers.

What other wild animals were around? Jack wouldn't have been surprised to see a shark cruise by the raft. For all he knew, Himalayan river sharks might be terrorizing villagers all the way to Kathmandu. There were probably piranhas somewhere. One minute, he and Harry would be sitting on the raft; the next, they'd be just a pile of gnawed bones at the bottom of the river.

Why did his parents always take him places where a person could be killed in a bizarre animal attack? What did they have against Rome or Paris? Nobody ever got attacked by a crocodile in any of Europe's famed historical cities.

"How're we gonna sleep tonight?" Harry asked. "I'll be freaking out every time I close my eyes, thinking one of those crocs is sneaking up on us."

"I'm pretty sure I saw on Animal Planet that crocodiles bury their eggs in sand. So if you're a crocodile and you see just rocks, you're going to think, 'This does not look like my regular habitat. I better go somewhere else.' We should be okay if we just climb up on a slope."

"Gotcha," Harry said.

Jack paused. "Harry, do you have any other

ideas? Because my last idea about camping on the sand wasn't very good."

Harry sat silent for a few minutes. Then he said, "Nope, I got nothing."

In the late afternoon, Jack pointed out a shallow cave within the stone cliffs, ten feet above the water's edge. If there were any crocodiles around, he didn't see how one could crawl up to it.

Jack steered the raft to the base of the slope and looped the bowline over a rock protruding from the water. He attached the monkey's Velcro paws around the raft rope and jumped onto the riverbank. Jack found chips in the rock to use as hand- and footholds. Harry climbed up after him.

The cave was five feet deep and nearly twenty feet wide. It wouldn't be comfortable to sleep in, but at least Jack and Harry had plenty of room to stretch out. The air was cooler than it had been earlier, and the cave felt damp. Jack pulled two long-sleeved T-shirts from his pack. They struggled to get Harry into one until Jack finally yanked it down around Harry's waist.

Harry looked at his chest. The shirt had a picture of a crown on the front. Underneath, it said *Keep Calm and Carry On*.

"I didn't buy them," Jack said, looking at his own shirt. It had a picture of a unicorn and the phrase *I'M A BELIEVER*.

"Your mom?"

"Yup."

They watched the sun set over the mountains while eating titaura and listening to the gentle slap of waves against the sides of the raft.

Harry looked around the shallow cave and said, "If my parents could see where I'm sleeping tonight, they would totally freak out."

"Mine wouldn't."

Harry snorted. "Yeah, they would."

"My parents don't really freak out," Jack said.

Jack looked at Harry thoughtfully. As far as Jack could tell, Harry had made it to age eighteen without any scars or permanent disabilities. Harry said his parents were prone to freaking out. The Aiken children had mentioned that if they came home later than promised, their mom had a meltdown. And one time, when

Zack forgot to tell his mom that he was sleeping at Jack's house, Zack's mom had showed up and said she'd practically had a nervous breakdown. There had to be some kind of connection. All those other parents couldn't be wrong.

"So, Harry," Jack said. "What causes your parents to freak out?" If Jack could pick up the right tips from Harry, maybe Jack's parents could learn to freak out sometimes. "Do you know when they are about to freak out, or does it come on suddenly?"

"Mainly, they freak out about my future," Harry said. "One time, I heard my dad tell my mom they would be lucky if I didn't end up as a hobo. They say they want the best for me. But I'm like, dude, I don't want to go to Harvard."

Jack was mesmerized. Harry's parents were *for* going to Harvard and *against* being a hobo. Jack planned on going to Harvard himself, and he'd never had any interest whatsoever in the hobo lifestyle.

"What's wrong with Harvard?" Jack asked.

"It's what happens to you when you get out," Harry said. "All the sudden, you're in the world of business. But what are you going to do about it? You went to Harvard, so now you're a Harvard guy and you have to do Harvard stuff."

Jack thought he would love to be a Harvard guy and do Harvard stuff.

"If you could see the kind of thing my parents do at these executive training seminars," Harry said, "you wouldn't believe it."

"Like what?" Jack asked, propping his chin on his hand.

"They take these people into the forest and make them climb a pole, with only their group supporting them, for some kind of trust-building thing. But I'm like, if you don't already trust these guys, what are you doin' in the middle of the woods with them? They could be murderers."

Jack thought Harry was right about that. Every time some killer got arrested on the news, the neighbors always said they were shocked because he was such a quiet, friendly guy.

"Then the group pretends they've been in a plane crash and have to figure out which supplies to use to get rescued. And again, I'm like, dude, how many hours of everybody's life are you gonna waste arguing about what to do with the flares?"

Jack thought that the answer was obvious: wait until you hear a search helicopter and then shoot the flares off.

"Then a bus picks them up, and these guys are supposed to go back to the office and magically dominate the business world. My parents get paid to do that every weekend. When I was younger, I used to have to go with them."

Jack thought it sounded like an ideal childhood—parents insisting on an Ivy League education, organized camping trips in the well-maintained forests of Connecticut.

Harry glanced at Jack and laughed. "They'd love a kid like you. The kind of kid that worries about empty calories. Not like the kid they got. When I told my mom and dad I was using the money I inherited from my uncle to travel around the world and find myself, they said they were disappointed. Like, 'We gave you every opportunity in the world, and this is what you're doing?'"

Jack sat up. "You know, Harry, I just thought of something. What if we traded for a while? Then your parents could have the kid of their dreams. My parents couldn't care less if you went to Harvard. It wouldn't be a permanent switch, and we could still see our real parents on holidays and summer vacations."

"I doubt my parents would go for something like that," Harry said. "They're always worried about what the neighbors would say. And anyway, all I know about your parents is that they invented a religion, knocked me off a truck, and might be paragliding around the mountains looking for us."

"That's all true, but my parents would never be disappointed in you," Jack said. "Over the summer, I came in dead last in a swim meet. My mom and dad took me out to dinner to celebrate. They even ordered a cake that said, *Jack Berenson, Olympic Champion*. I was sure they hadn't actually seen the race until my mom showed me the video. Harry, you could do anything, and my parents would be proud of you."

"Anything?"

"Absolutely anything. And just think, you've been traveling all over the world trying to find yourself. My parents love to travel, so you could have company while you're looking. And while you're traveling with *my* parents, I'll be at *your* parent's house, following all their rules and doing my homework. It's a win for everybody."

"It sounds good, but it would never work," Harry said. "Nobody just decides to switch kids."

"But it's something to think about, right?" Jack said.

"Yeah," Harry said, nodding his head. "I guess there's nothing wrong with thinking about something."

"I know it would be an unusual switch," Jack said. "But considering our situations, it's probably the most logical thing to do."

Jack felt a twinge of guilt when he imagined telling his parents that he'd be moving to Connecticut. But then he could break it to them gently by saying, "Just pretend I'm lost. The time will fly by and before you know it, it will be Christmas."

He could see Zack and Diana over summer vacation and holidays. After all, he wasn't seeing them more often than that now.

Jack fell asleep imagining romping through the forests of Connecticut and sitting around a cozy campfire, talking about Harvard.

● ● ●

Rain pounded down outside the cave, soaking through Jack's sneakers. He sat up and pulled his legs in. Water poured over the edge of the overhang in a solid sheet. Bright flashes of lightning lit up the wall of water.

Harry snored next to him. Jack supposed Harry could sleep through the end of the world if he felt like it.

"Harry," Jack said, shaking his shoulder. "Wake up."

Harry stretched his legs, pulled his feet in, and said, "Raining? Seriously?"

They sat for hours, listening to cracks of thunder and watching streaks of lightning. The wind whipped through the canyon, producing a ghostly *haaaaaaa-hooooooooo*.

By midday, the downpour became a drizzle and the sky cleared to an overcast gray.

Jack peered down at the river. It had swollen and turned brown. The raft bounced up and down on roiling waves.

"That doesn't look good," Harry said.

"What should we do?" Jack asked.

"I don't know."

"We could wait for the river to go down, but that could take days. Or we could try to hike out. Only, we don't know where the road is and we might get lost. We could end up like those people in the Andes who had to eat each other to stay alive. Not that I would ever do that. No matter how hungry I got."

Harry shook his head. "I can't be that guy who was trying to find himself but ended up eating his buddy instead. I just can't be that guy."

"I think we should keep going on the raft and be really careful about watching what's ahead," Jack said. "After all, we're more seasoned rafters now."

"That's true," Harry said. "We're getting pretty good at it."

"And Mr. Shrestha said there was a sign for Shangrilala. I feel like we must be getting close to it."

* * *

The raft bounced up and down. Jack held the bow steady while Harry jumped on. They pulled their long-sleeved shirts off and put them in Jack's pack to stay dry. After they had secured all the supplies, Jack stuffed Mack the monkey into a plastic bag, tying the ends of the bag to the rope on the raft.

After Jack and Harry had secured their life vests, Jack wrestled with the equipment bag and pulled the helmets out. "Here, Harry," Jack said, passing one to Harry. "We probably won't need them, but it's better to be on the safe side."

Harry looked at the helmet and laughed. "I'm not putting that thing on."

"Harry, head injuries can be devastating," Jack said. "That's why helmets got invented.

One bad decision could ruin the rest of your life. You could die. Or you could lose your memory. You could get paralyzed."

Harry held his hands up. As he tightened his chin strap, he muttered, "We look like two old ladies."

"Two old, *safe* ladies."

Jack untied the boat and grabbed an oar. He and Harry tried to paddle toward the middle of the river, but the current pulled them downstream. The boat spun and rode down the river backwards.

"We have to turn it around," Jack said.

Jack and Harry dug their paddles into the water. The raft seemed to slow down, but the paddles weren't turning them around.

The raft rolled down into white water and then popped up again.

Jack tried paddling backward, while Harry paddled forward, and the raft slowly turned.

Once the bow faced downstream, Jack moved to the rear of the boat. While Harry paddled, Jack called out "paddle left" or "paddle right" to steer them around boulders sticking out of the water. He tried to keep the raft in the middle of the river and away from the shallow, rocky shore.

The river narrowed as the day wore on. Jack and Harry began to pass scattered boulders poking out of the water, hazards they had to paddle around or push off from. Swirling dips pulled the boat down and then spat it back up. Each time the raft dropped, Jack felt his stomach lurch.

"How long can this go on?" Harry shouted from the front of the boat.

Jack stood up to get a better view of what was ahead.

Two hundred yards downstream, the river funneled between two massive boulders. Beyond it, white spray flew high into the air.

"Paddle right!" Jack shouted to Harry. "To the rocks!"

They dug their paddles in, toward flat rocks at the side of the canyon. The raft flew past the bank they had aimed for and spun like a top.

Harry cried. "We're going down!"

The raft sailed over the waterfall.

Jack felt as though his insides were in the wrong place. Maybe his stomach had taken a look over the precipice and decided to wait at the top. Jack grabbed the rope that ran around the sides of the raft and braced himself.

The boat flipped as it hit the white water at the bottom of the waterfall. Jack was pushed under. He couldn't tell which way was up or down. When he let go of the rope and popped to the surface, waves crashed over his head, and his life jacket banged up against a boulder. The current whipped him downstream.

Jack struggled to turn himself so he could see where he was going. He forced his legs out to push off oncoming rocks. Ahead of him, the overturned raft bounced on top of the waves.

Jack was swept down a series of rapids. Choking on the water, he washed into a flat section of river and angled himself to the riverbank.

He lay there, heaving and looking around for the raft.

It had disappeared. So had Harry.

"Harry!" Jack's voice bounced off the canyon

walls. "Harry, where are you?"

He stumbled along the bank, climbing over boulders. The path he took was as full of twists as the river. Each time Jack thought he might find a good view around a bend, he just found another turn. After an hour, he spotted the yellow paddle end of an oar lying on a pile of rocks. Jack picked it up; it was the only sign of the raft he had found so far.

The sun passed over the cliffs, and shadows descended on the canyon. Jack staggered on until twilight. A chill settled into his bones. He crept up the slope of the riverbank and lay down on a flat boulder. The stone was still warm from the sun.

Each time Jack closed his eyes, all he could see was Harry. Harry thinking the rafting trip would be an adventure. Harry trusting Jack about which fork in the river to take. But they had taken the wrong fork; Jack was sure of it.

The night crept on, the stone cooling underneath Jack, and a light breeze chilling him to the bone. Finally, the sky lightened to pink.

Jack staggered to his feet, his muscles

cramped from the cold. He drank water from the river and set off over the rocks. By midmorning he was hot and sweaty.

Jack sat down on a boulder to rest. He couldn't stop thinking about what might have happened to Harry. Maybe he had drowned.

But maybe Harry was fine and just . . . just what? If Harry were fine, Jack would have found him by now.

Harry wasn't fine. He was gone.

Because Jack had been wrong. Wrong about buying the raft, wrong about sleeping on the sand, and wrong about the fork in the river.

Harry had said he trusted in Jack's superior knowledge of the wilderness. Except, Jack didn't have any superior knowledge.

"I'm always telling my mom and dad to be careful," Jack whispered. "To stop making bad decisions. But it turns out I'm just like them."

Jack dragged himself to his feet. He would have to call Harry's parents when he got back to civilization. Jack would have to tell them that Harry hadn't found himself after all. Harry just had the bad luck to find a Berenson.

CHAPTER 7

In which the ship goes down

All Jack could do was push on. He climbed over rocks and waded through shallows until in the late afternoon, he scrambled around a bend in the river.

"Jack!" Harry cried. "Dude! I thought you were dead!"

Harry stood on a rubbly bank next to the raft. Jack's monkey hung from a tree, river water dripping from its fur.

"Harry! I thought *you* were dead!" Jack scrambled over the rocks. "But how? I thought you drowned! How did you—"

"I was stuck underneath the raft with my arm tangled in the rope," Harry said. "I got it free. Then all the sudden the raft was gone. I got slammed in the head. When I came to, I was by myself. I found the raft up on the rocks."

"But I walked pretty far yesterday. Today I walked almost the whole day," Jack said. "How did you get so far down the river?"

Harry held his hands up. "Totally my bad. I figured you were ahead of me, so I got on the raft and tried to catch up to you. I finally gave up and stopped here. I was getting seriously bummed about having to tell your mom and dad you were dead. That is exactly the kind of thing parents are not gonna want to hear."

Jack felt like a bag full of bricks had slid off his shoulders. Harry wasn't dead. Harry was standing right there. Totally alive. Jack supposed this was how his parents felt each time they found him after losing him: "Yes, we're idiots, but look at you, you rascal! You survived!"

● ● ●

Jack and Harry spent the rest of the afternoon drying out. Jack's pack was gone, lost somewhere in the river. They hung their T-shirts on scraggily bushes. Jack laid the plastic bags with the supplies on warm rocks to dry and wrung the water out of Mack the monkey. Harry found dry kindling for a campfire.

Jack climbed up the slope to scout downstream. Once he scrambled back down, he told Harry, "It looks like we've been through the worst of it. From what I can see, the river is rough, but no more waterfalls."

Harry held the pot over the fire, boiling Wai Wai noodles. "Flying over a waterfall is the kind of thing that's hilarious to tell people at a party, but not hilarious to actually live through."

"Harry, when you tell the story at a party, you can say it was my fault. I'm sure I picked the wrong fork in the river. We won't find Shangrilala going this way."

"Uh, I kind of guessed that after yesterday. But, dude, you were right about the road being on the south side of the river. All that time on the bus, it was right out the window. So I kinda think we'll have to run into it. I mean, wilderness can't go on forever, right?"

Harry was right. They might not find Shangrilala, but sooner or later, they were bound to see the road.

Jack set a bowl from the mess kit close to the campfire and leaned the damp monkey up against it for a picture.

Harry glanced at Mack, who now appeared to be supervising the cooking. "What did you say you were supposed to be doing with that thing?" he asked.

"Gnoming," Jack said, pulling the disposable camera from its ziplock bag. "You bring something on a trip, like a lawn gnome, then take pictures of it." He snapped a picture.

"Gnoming," Harry said. "That's cool. Our neighbors in Connecticut have a ceramic squirrel on their roof. I should have brought it with me."

"But that would be stealing," Jack said.

Harry snorted. "Wow, you sound like my dad."

That was the second time Harry had compared Jack to an older relative. "Harry,"

Jack said, "do you think I act older than I am?"

Harry stirred the Wai Wai noodles and said, "No offense, but it wouldn't kill you to chill out a little."

Jack felt his face burn.

"Sorry, I take that back," Harry said. "I shouldn't be telling anybody else what to do. I can't even figure out what I'm supposed to do."

"It seems like it should be easy to find yourself, Harry," Jack said. "Everybody is good at something."

Harry dished out the Wai Wai noodles. "Yeah. It's finding the something that's the hard part."

"Well," Jack said between bites, "let's see. You have a very relaxed personality. Except for when you're around crocodiles or flying over a waterfall, but those kinds of things don't come up every day. You're friendly. You love sugar. I mean, how many packs of titaura did you buy? You would probably eat it all day long if you could. You don't want to go to Harvard or follow in your parent's footsteps. And you like to travel. So really, all you have to do is find a job where you can relax, be friendly, travel from place to place, and eat a lot of sugar."

"No wonder I have to wander all over the planet. A job like that is gonna be hard to find," Harry said.

Jack finished his noodles and lay next to the campfire, trying to imagine Harry's dream job.

"Really, I just like to make people happy," Harry said. "That makes me happy. If I could figure out the whole world peace thing, I would totally do it. Or if I could end world hunger. 'Boom. Nobody is hungry, starting now.'"

Jack thought taking on world peace and ending hunger were noble causes but didn't really sound like entry-level jobs.

"Harry! Why don't you own your own ice-cream truck? Ice cream is full of sugar. You could drive around from place to place, making people happy *and* solving their hunger. You'd only have to work in the summer, and then you could travel anywhere you wanted in the winter. You wouldn't have to go to Harvard. And if you do decide to switch parents, I know you'd have my parent's full support. They'd probably wonder why they didn't think of it."

Harry rolled over. "I like ice cream. I like kids too. And I always liked it when the ice-cream truck came down my street in the summer. I used to go under all the couch cushions to make sure I had enough change for one of those cones with the chocolate and nuts on top."

"Just think, Harry," Jack said. "As the owner, you could eat those cones all day long if you felt like it."

"I could call my truck The Wandering Cone."

"Your logo could be a cone with feet," Jack said.

Harry high-fived Jack and said, "Dude, I'm found!"

Jack fell asleep while Harry strategized the launching of The Wandering Cone.

■ ■ ■

Jack and Harry set off at dawn. The river was rough, and they periodically pulled the raft up on the banks just to catch their breath. So far, they hadn't seen any sign of the road.

As the raft barreled toward another series of steep rapids, Jack spotted them too late. "Hold on, Harry," he yelled.

The raft slid down the nearest rapid. It felt like the Raptor Roller Coaster Jack went on every summer. Every year, Jack told himself that now that he was older, the ride would probably be fun, and every year he ended up embarrassing himself by screaming, "Get me off this thing!"

The raft turned sideways as it slid down another chute. Harry hung over the side of the boat. Jack grabbed the back of his pants and hauled him back in.

The raft crashed down onto a boulder and bounced off. Jack watched the sides of the raft shrinking. A patch had blown. They were about to go down with the ship. "Harry, we're sinking!"

"What?" Harry cried.

"Sinking!"

"Swim for it, Harry," Jack cried.

"Swim where?" Harry shrieked.

Jack jumped clear of the raft. A giant wave pushed him forward. He couldn't steer himself; he was going too fast.

Jack aimed himself at a large boulder near the closest riverbank and let the rushing water push him up the rock until he could grab hold of an overhanging tree branch. He hauled himself onto dry land. The raft was a few yards away, deflated and tangled in a pile of dead tree branches.

Harry was upstream, scrambling over rocks along the opposite bank of the river.

"Jack!" Harry cried, over the roar of the river.

"Harry!" Jack yelled back. "What are you doing over there?"

"Standing here. What are you doing over there?"

Jack realized he was the one on the wrong side of the river—the north side. Harry was on the south.

"Harry," Jack yelled. "Stay where you are. I'll go higher and see if there's a better place to cross."

Harry gave him the thumbs-up.

Stunted trees with gnarled branches covered the slope of the gorge, their roots clutching rocks. Jack climbed up, pulling himself from tree to tree. Once he was high enough, he turned around.

From where he stood, the gorge went on forever. Across the river and up the slope from where Harry stood, a canyon wall rose up steeply. Beyond that, a thick pine forest carpeted the land. No sign of the road.

Jack slipped and slid down the incline, grabbing at tree branches to slow his descent.

"Harry," Jack yelled. "I can't see the road, but it has to be there somewhere. If you can climb to the top of the cliff and head straight in from where you are, you might be able to find it and get help."

"How are you going to cross the river?" Harry shouted.

"I can't," Jack yelled. "You'll have to leave me behind."

"No way," Harry said. "I'm not leaving my number one dude."

Jack was touched. He had not known he was Harry's number one dude. But Harry really would have to go. "You've got to do it," Jack shouted.

Harry sat down on a slab of stone and crossed his arms.

Harry wasn't going. Now what?

If Jack's mom and dad were stranded on a riverside slope somewhere, they would probably just dive into the water; try to swim for it; realize that was hopeless; and then, as they were swept away, shout, "A bit of a mishap, darling! We'll be back directly!"

So that was out.

Jack examined the river. It wasn't wide, but that was part of the problem. The water was funneling through the narrow gorge as if someone had turned a tap on full blast.

Jack looked at the deflated raft. He could detach the rope that ran around it, throw it to Harry, and have Harry pull him across . . . but all he could imagine was disappearing downstream, dragging the rope and Harry behind him. Any plan that involved being in the water wouldn't be a good plan.

Jack climbed down to the raft and hauled it higher onto the bank. Now that it had deflated, it felt ten times heavier. Jack pulled Mack the monkey out of the plastic bag that was still tied to the rope and then turned the raft over. A patch dangled off the rubber.

The rope attached to the top of the raft was double looped. If the rope could reach across the river, maybe he could construct some kind of tightrope over to the other side.

Jack followed the rope until he found where its two ends tied together. The first knot would have been enough to keep it secured; the other fourteen were a series of weird loops and braids, shrunk tight by repeated soaking in water and drying in the sun. Jack could picture Mr. Shrestha chuckling to himself and thinking no lactose-intolerant American would ever get it untied.

Jack worked through the knots until he yanked the rope free. He grabbed a rock the size of his fist and carefully tied the rope around it.

Harry stood on the opposite bank, shading his eyes.

"Harry," Jack said. "I'm going to throw the rope. When you get it, tie it to a sturdy tree, as high off the ground as you can."

Harry shouted, "Go for it."

Jack pulled his arm back, aimed for Harry, and pitched the rock.

The rock sailed over the water but fell short of the other bank. Jack pulled the rope back to his side, the rock still tied to the throwing end.

"Good try, dude," Harry said. "You can do it. Huck it like you mean it."

"Like I mean it," Jack whispered.

The rock landed just shy of the other bank. Harry leaned over the water and scooped it up. He held it over his head. "Got it!"

"You tie the rope first," Jack called. "Then I'll tie it on this side."

Harry scrambled to the highest tree on the banks, while Jack fed him more rope. He hoped Harry was good with knots. Jack only knew one. Zack's dad had taught him how to tie a bowline when they had gone camping.

Harry came back to the riverbank and gave Jack the thumbs-up.

Jack wrapped his end of the rope around the sturdiest-looking tree he could reach, while repeating Zack's dad's directions. "Loop around and then the rabbit comes up the hole and it runs around the rope-tree and then back down the hole."

Jack pulled the rope tight. It *looked* like a bowline, anyway. When he tested the tension, the rope felt springy in his hand. Down at the bank of the river, the rope stretched a few feet over Jack's head. He looked across the water. He would have to inch across like an upside-down caterpillar. It was one thing to say he would dangle over a wild river, Jack realized, and another to actually get started.

Well, he thought, Harry had told him to chill out. He supposed now would be a good time to start.

Jack hooked the monkey's paws around his neck, grabbed the rope, and swung his legs up.

CHAPTER 8

In which an exit strategy does not go as planned

Jack swayed over the river. He pulled himself forward, hand over hand, his legs wrapped around the rope. He could already feel the burn in his arms. Endurance wasn't going to be his strong suit.

He inched along and felt the rope sag. The river rushed just below him.

"Keep going, Jack," Harry called. "You're at the halfway mark."

Only halfway? Jack's arms were on fire. If he had been in gym class, it would be the moment Jack would have fallen to the mat, stood up, and said, "Just got over the flu."

"C'mon, Jack. You can do it!"

Jack turned his head to glance at the river surging underneath him. He squeezed his eyes shut and pulled himself forward. He felt his legs slipping from the rope.

"You're almost there," Harry called.

Suddenly, Harry had him by the shoulders. They tumbled onto the stony beach.

Jack crouched on his hands and knees, catching his breath. The middle of the rope grazed the water. Harry slapped Jack on the back a couple of times.

A cool breeze whipped down the canyon. Jack and Harry were both soaked. Jack shivered against the fading afternoon sun. "Harry," he said, "it's too late to try to climb the canyon and search for the road. I think we're stuck here for the night."

Harry nodded. "All we got left is the titaura I had in my pocket. The chili stuff."

Jack and Harry huddled under an overhang nearby and chewed chili titaura. Jack's mouth felt like somebody had thrown a lit firecracker into it, but the chili pepper sent warm waves through his body.

Harry rubbed his arms and said, "You know, when you think about it, it's almost unbelievable that we're huddling under a cliff in Nepal somewhere, totally lost, all because your parents decided to start their own religion."

"It should be unbelievable," Jack said, "but considering the other schemes they've come up with, I'm not that surprised. My parent's motto should be: '*Expect* the unbelievable.'"

"What are you gonna do when you see them?" Harry asked.

"I'm running out of ideas," Jack said. "Lecturing doesn't work. It's just in one ear and out the other. I wrote family rules, but they didn't work. So then I figured the real problem was instincts. That their parent instincts were lying in them dormant because they hadn't been used. If I could just get the instincts to come out, everything would be fine. Now, I'm worried they might not actually have any."

"You never know what Mother Nature will come up with," Harry said. "In second grade,

I went to school with a kid who had different colored eyes. One was blue, and the other one was green. I thought he might be an alien."

"Even if I go and live with your parents in Connecticut, I still have to stay alive through holidays and summer vacation. Maybe I should try grounding my mom and dad." Jack said.

"Would they go for that?" Harry asked.

"They might. They're pretty agreeable."

"I don't know," Harry said. "Grounding never changed me. I just used the alone time to play video games."

Jack could imagine his parents doing some version of that. He knew from experience that they would play Bananagrams all day long if they were allowed to. Since he would still have to visit his parents during the holidays, he would have to hone his survival skills. He decided he'd write the United States Marines and ask for advice. Or for a Marines handbook. He might even ask for an actual Marine.

As the sun set, Jack curled up and watched the stars as Harry talked into the night.

"The first thing I'm gonna do when we get

back is learn how to make my own ice cream so I can invent original Wandering Cone flavors," Harry said. "I still got a lot of my inheritance money, so that should buy me a truck." Harry looked up to the sky and whispered, "Thanks, Uncle Dave."

"I'll paint a map of the world on the outside of the truck," he continued. "Then I'll paint little ice-cream cones on the map for everywhere I've been. Then I'll name all my flavors after different places. Like, for the Kathmandu Kamikaze, I'm gonna fill the bottom of the cone with chocolate syrup, then add vanilla ice cream. The kid will get to the bottom and be like, whoa, there's chocolate in here—bonus. And instead of just a bell, I'm going to record an original song. I already thought up some of the lyrics. You want to hear it?"

"Absolutely," Jack said, hugging his arms against the cold.

"This is what I got so far," Harry said. He cleared his throat.

"The Wandering Cone wanders here and there, looking for kids 'cause it's got ice cream to share. If you got no money, I'll give you credit, 'cause you can tell your parents later and get it. The owner of the truck is a friendly dude, lookin' for dudes with good attitudes. No adults wanted who say life is a bummer, only happy dudes, 'cause, hey, dude, it's summer!"

Jack would not personally have used so many *dudes*. But the song really did reflect Harry's cheerful personality. "Harry, I would definitely buy ice cream from The Wandering Cone."

"It's easy when you're doing something you love."

As the night wore on, Harry alerted Jack whenever he had thought of a new Wandering Cone flavor. The Bangkok Freeze would be mango and pineapple mixed together and topped with shredded coconut. Jack fell asleep while Harry worked out the Mumbai Madness.

● ● ●

The next morning, Jack surveyed the canyon walls to figure out the best way up. The cliff was rugged and uneven. Jack spotted plenty of hand- and footholds, but he could just imagine getting halfway up to the top and finding out he had run out of places to grip.

"Harry," Jack said. "Look over there. To the right. I think we could get to the top from that way. Do you think we should try?"

Harry shrugged. "You decide. I'm an ice-cream guy. You got a question about sugar cones versus waffle cones, I'm your man. But rock climbing? I got nothing."

"Okay..." Jack said. "Then I guess we'll try it."

They made their way over to the right side of the cliff. Jack stuck his foot in the first indentation. It was deep enough for his whole sneaker.

"I'll go first," Jack said.

He stepped up and clutched at a handhold above his head. "You'll have to steady yourself with your hands." He hoisted himself to the next foothold, found another handhold, and climbed upward. He didn't dare look down. "How's it going, Harry?"

"Going okay," Harry said.

Harry didn't sound as though he was right behind Jack.

"Are you climbing?" Jack asked.

"Not yet. Soon, though."

Jack supposed Harry wanted some space between them in case they had to edge themselves back down the cliff.

Jack climbed to what he thought was the halfway point. His left foot was braced in one of the holes. He had to stretch his right leg all the way out to jam it into the next hole. Jack pushed himself up. He wobbled and clutched at a protruding piece of stone. As he steadied himself, he shouted, "Watch out for this part, Harry! I almost fell."

Harry's voice sounded distant and high. "Almost fell?"

Jack reached the top of the cliff and pulled himself onto a plateau scattered with rubble and hemmed in by tall pines. He turned around and peered over the side of the cliff.

Harry hadn't left the beach. His face was ashen as he stared up at Jack.

"Harry," Jack called. "What are you doing?"

"Standing on the beach," Harry called back.

"No," Jack yelled, "I mean why aren't you climbing?"

"I can't."

"Are you afraid of heights?" Jack shouted.

"No," Harry said, "I'm afraid of falling from heights!"

"But, Harry, you have to climb up. There's no other way out."

"Can't! The Wandering Cone will have to go on without me."

Jack did not think The Wandering Cone was going anywhere without Harry.

Jack stared down at Harry, wondering how to get him up the cliff. He didn't have any equipment. Just the clothes he was wearing and a bedraggled stuffed monkey.

"Harry," Jack called, unhooking the monkey and laying him on the ground, "I'll talk you through it."

He lowered himself down on his stomach and hung over the side of the cliff. The view to the bottom of the canyon made his head spin.

Below him, Harry paced on the sand, running a hand through his hair.

"You can do it, Harry. I'll guide you step-by-step, exactly how I got up here."

Harry stopped pacing. "Okay, but don't let me fall!"

Jack decided not to mention there was no actual way for him to stop Harry from falling. "See that crevice in the rock right in front of you? And then there's a handhold to the right? That's where you start."

Jack directed Harry, crevice by crevice, up the cliff. At the halfway mark, Harry's shaky

voice drifted up to him. "I'm at the bad part," Harry said.

"Don't be nervous," Jack called. "Your arms and legs are longer than mine. You'll be all right. Just stretch your right leg out."

Harry stretched his right leg out, and it dangled in the air.

"Feel for the hole with the tip of your sneaker," Jack said.

Harry rubbed the end of his shoe along the rock face and then slipped it into the hole.

"Yes, that's it. Now just push yourself up," Jack shouted.

Jack squeezed his eyes shut. He couldn't watch.

Harry screamed.

Jack's heart stopped beating. He opened his eyes, expecting to see Harry's broken body sprawled on the beach.

Harry scaled the last few feet, climbing fast with a wild look in his eyes.

Jack reached down for Harry and pulled him over the top.

"Why did you scream?" Jack cried. "I thought you fell!"

"I screamed because I almost fell," Harry said, gasping.

Jack grabbed the monkey, and they crawled away from the cliff. They sat in the sunshine while Harry caught his breath.

Jack knew the river ran west to east, and the road ran along with it, on the south side of the river. Jack figured if they headed straight into the pines, they were bound to find it. Eventually.

"We have to go this way, Harry," Jack said,

pointing to the trees. "We'll use the sun to make sure we keep heading in the right direction."

Jack looked up to the sky. It was probably around eight o'clock in the morning. "The sun will head west, so we just keep it on our left until midday, then on the right after that and we should be okay."

Harry nodded. Jack hung the monkey around his neck, and they entered the forest. The trees were dense, and the silence was unnerving. Jack could hear Harry breathing behind him. It felt like the loneliest place on Earth.

Jack paused occasionally to peer up at the sun, barely visible through the towering pines. He held his hand out, and Harry stopped.

"Wait. Do you hear that?" Jack asked.

A sound like a vacuum cleaner filled the forest.

"What is it?" Harry asked.

"I don't know," Jack said, clutching Harry's arm, "but whatever it is, it's some kind of machine, and that means people!"

They raced toward the sound, jumping over fallen tree trunks and ducking under branches.

The sound grew louder. Jack could not identify it. It sputtered and hiccoughed, making a *krump-kerwump* sound.

"I bet it's loggers using some kind of machine to chop up wood," Jack said.

"I think you're right," Harry said.

The sound stopped. Jack and Harry stood motionless, listening.

When the sound started again, Jack tiptoed forward and peeked around a tree.

A beast resembling a bear crouched twenty feet from where Jack stood. It had a rangy build and a long black mane framing its face. It held down a rotten tree branch with long, curved claws and nosed through the crumbling wood.

Harry whispered, "Yeti!"

The beast turned toward the sound of Harry's voice and stood up on its hind legs.

Jack grabbed Harry's arm. "Run!"

Jack and Harry crashed through the forest. Tree branches grabbed at Jack's T-shirt and scratched his arms. Harry's heavy footsteps pounded behind him. They ran for a quarter of an hour, until Jack couldn't go any farther. He glanced over his shoulder. The beast, whatever it had been, was gone.

Jack bent over, hands on his knees, gasping for breath.

Harry leaned on a tree trunk. "Jack, we're lost in a forest with a Yeti. And when the sun goes down, we'll be lost in a forest with a Yeti *in the dark*."

"It wasn't a Yeti, Harry. It was some kind of bear. Some kind of bear that just . . . doesn't look exactly like other bears."

"Nobody ever believes the stories until it's too late," Harry said.

"Whatever it is, all we can do is keep going. C'mon, we have to stay on the move."

They jogged through the forest until they reached a small clearing. The brush on one side had been trampled down. Another bear was around somewhere.

Jack put his hand on Harry's arm and pointed to it, then laid a finger over his lips. He cautiously approached the trampled underbrush and moved a branch aside to get a better view.

"Harry," Jack cried, "it's a path!"

Past the pine branches overhead, a wide trail snaked through the forest.

"Oh, no," Harry said. "They actually have paths? How many Yetis are there around here?"

Jack bent down and examined the ground. "Look there, right in the dirt. That's a sneaker print."

"Yetis don't wear sneakers," Harry said in a hopeful voice.

"No, they don't," Jack said.

"A path has to go somewhere, right?" Harry asked. "I feel like if we can just not get attacked by an enraged Yeti, we might be all right. We just gotta not disturb the habitat."

"I'm sure of it, Harry. All paths go somewhere. That's the whole point of a path. Let's go!"

As they ran down the twisting trail, Harry said, "When we get back to civilization, I'll break it to your parents that I'm excommunicating myself from Nosnereb. I'm gonna be totally focused on The Wandering Cone."

"I really think The Wandering Cone is going to be a big success," Jack said. "And if we trade parents for a while, which I hope you're still considering, I know my mom and dad will be happy to help you get your business going."

Harry grabbed Jack's arm. "Dude, look!"

They had come to the top of a gentle slope. A town crowded with one-story cement buildings stretched out below them, curving around a large lake.

Jack and Harry scrambled down to the dusty road that led into the town.

"The first thing we'll do is find a restaurant and eat," Jack said. "Eat a lot. We could even eat twice if we feel like it. I still have a lot of my mom's traveler's checks in my pocket. They're kind of damp, but I figure they'll still work. Food is on me. Or on my mom."

Jack and Harry passed a Nepalese man wearing a sporty yellow baseball cap. "Hello," Jack said.

The man stared at him.

"Oh, sorry. I meant, *Namaste.*"

Turning back to Harry, Jack said, "We'll find a phone and call the US Embassy. I'm sure they'll be able to help us."

Jack and Harry walked farther along, passing small shops selling used clothes, kitchenware, and religious statues. No food. They stopped in the middle of a dusty intersection.

"Which way, dude?" Harry said.

"I don't know," Jack said. He turned 360 degrees, looking for restaurant signs.

"Wait a minute," Jack said. "Look at that group of men over there. Why are they staring at us?"

A group of seven or eight men crowded in front of a shopwindow, peering at a notice and turning to point at Jack and Harry.

"And that guy with the yellow baseball cap. Wasn't he the guy we passed when we came into town?"

"Maybe they're not used to seeing tourists," Harry said.

"Maybe."

Jack squinted at the piece of paper the men were staring at.

"Harry," Jack said. "The poster in that window—there's a picture of me and a hand-drawn sketch that sort of looks like you."

"That totally makes sense," Harry said. "See, dude, your parents aren't as bad as you thought. Putting up a missing child poster is exactly the kind of thing any responsible parent would do. It's like they went straight for the Amber Alert."

"That really is something a regular parent would do," Jack said, a little surprised. "Maybe my mom and dad have finally found their parent instincts. C'mon, let's go."

Jack and Harry walked toward the group of men. "Yes," Jack called. "You are correct—it's us! We're found!"

The men ran toward them, shouting in Nepali.

"Why are they yelling like that?"

"I don't know," Harry cried, "but they look mad!"

"Run!" Jack yelled.

Jack and Harry sprinted down the road and ducked into a narrow alley. The alleyway ended at a brick wall, with two narrow passageways veering off in opposite directions.

"This way," Jack said, turning to the right.

Jack and Harry made two more turns with the men in pursuit. They skidded to a stop in front of another brick wall. A dead end. Jack turned around and cried, "We come in peace! We're just tourists!"

The men closest to Jack and Harry blocked their escape. One of them threw a ball of paper at Jack's feet. In the distance, other men shouted for the police.

Jack bent down and picked it up, smoothing out the crumpled paper. His school picture, the one Jack's dad kept in his wallet, had been enlarged and printed on the top left of the page. A drawing that looked as though a kindergartner had done it was next to the photo. The only way Jack could even tell it was supposed to be Harry was by the wild hair. Below the pictures, there was a paragraph of Nepali text, and below that, an English translation:

WANTED

Have you seen these men? Both are wanted in connection with a multimillion franc bank heist in Zurich. Reward is offered by the Swiss authorities for information leading to arrest and conviction. Use extreme caution in approaching these individuals. They are considered armed and dangerous.

"Is that us?" Harry asked in the high voice.

"Technically," Jack said. "But I'm sure it's just some kind of mix-up."

"Like what?" Harry shrieked. "What mix-up?"

Jack pondered what could account for him and Harry being identified as bank robbers. "Well, maybe the people at the printers messed up the photos on the flyers. So we ended up on this one, and the bank robbers are on the missing child poster."

"Dude," Harry said, "do you know what the prisons are like here?"

Jack did not. But as three armed policemen were making their way through the crowd, he assumed he was about to find out.

CHAPTER 9

In which Jack is introduced to his first prison cell

In the interrogation room, Jack began to lose faith in his "mix-up at the printer" theory.

The police chief leaned back in his chair. "There is no use in claiming you are innocent. We have proof."

"Proof?" Jack said. "But that's impossible. Harry and I have been rafting on the river, not robbing a Swiss bank."

"Dude," Harry said to the police chief.

The chief glared at him.

"Sorry," Harry said. "I mean, *officer*, I've never even been to Switzerland. I'm on a trip around the world to find myself. Nobody goes to Switzerland for that."

The chief cracked his knuckles and motioned for a guard. "Take them to a holding cell until we have confirmed their identities."

Jack and Harry were led to a small cell. The guard removed their handcuffs, pushed them inside, and threw Mack the monkey in after them. The cell door clanged shut. Jack and Harry sat on the floor, staring at each other.

Jack shifted on the damp cement. "Harry," Jack said, "I think Mr. Shrestha is behind this. I mean, he's the only person we've even seen."

"Why would Mr. Shrestha smash my dreams like that?" Harry said. "What's he got against a guy from Connecticut?"

Jack had one idea. "Mr. Shrestha wants revenge. Just think, Harry, first he had to deal with those lactose-intolerant Americans. Then we come along and bargain so hard for the raft. Remember? He wanted $5,000 for it, and we only gave him $300. We should have known he would hold a grudge."

"I bet they don't need ice cream in prison,"

Harry said softly. "Not even a Kathmandu Kamikaze."

Hours passed before the guard returned, unlocked the door, and said, "Come. The witnesses are here."

Jack scrambled to his feet. As he and Harry followed the guard down the dank halls, Jack whispered, "Witnesses! How could they have witnesses? And more than one? Do you suppose Mr. Shrestha is part of some kind of gang?"

"It's probably the lady from the shop," Harry said.

"The lady from the shop," Jack said. "I would never have suspected her."

The guard opened the door to a small, square room with walls covered in speckles of black mold. On one side, metal bars ran from floor to ceiling. A shade on the other side flew up. Jack's mom and dad stood behind another set of bars, with the police chief standing behind them.

"There you are, luv," his mom said.

"Claire, didn't I tell you the boy would be fine?" his dad said.

The police chief looked back and forth at Richard and Claire Berenson.

"Dad," Jack said, "we're not fine. The police think we robbed a bank! They said they have witnesses!"

"The great thing about witnesses, Son," Jack's dad said, "is that they can always recant their story. Happens every day."

"That's right," his mom said. "Recant. It's practically a witness tradition."

Jack narrowed his eyes.

"You?" he cried.

"Now, Jack," his mom said, "don't get hysterical. It seemed like a good idea at the time."

The police chief stepped forward. "Son? Recant? What is going on? Have you lied to the police?"

Jack's dad turned to the chief. "Now, officer, *lied* is a strong word. Let's say we were just a couple of desperate parents using a little... imagination."

"You see, sir," his mom said, "the one thing that makes Jack really mad is when we lose him. We swore we wouldn't let it happen again.

But then it *did* happen again, and we thought, no worries, let's paraglide over the mountains until we find them. Then we thought, hold on a minute, before we launch ourselves off a cliff, let's just pull out the old Berenson Family Decision-Making Rules to make sure we're on the right track. We asked ourselves, what would Jack do? So paragliding was out. Instead, we reported to one of your officers that Jack and Harry were missing, which is exactly the sort of thing Jack would do."

"But that fellow really didn't seem like he was on the case," his dad said. "So we thought, let's ramp this up a bit. Let's offer a reward."

"But, Jack," his mom said, "you had all the travelers' checks. We've had to panhandle to get by. We've begged coins off of nearly everybody in town. They'd all know we didn't have money for a reward."

"So then we thought, who *would* have a lot of money?" his dad asked.

"A Swiss bank, that's who."

"And then we thought, why would a Swiss bank offer a reward?"

"Because it was robbed."

"So you see, Son, it all just snowballed from there."

"That is the craziest thing I ever heard," Harry said.

"It's worse than you think," Jack said. "I didn't want to tell you while we were on the river because I wanted to keep your spirits up and also stay friends with you. But the thing that happened to your grandparents on that safari? It wasn't the Berensteins. It was the Berensons."

Harry reached through the bars and tried to grab Jack's dad. "You left my grandparents with a troop of wild baboons?"

"He must be talking about the Gradys," Jack's mom said. "Remember them, darling?"

"Remember them?" Jack's dad said. "It's almost like those people are haunting us."

"Haunting *you*?" Harry asked. "My grandma still has nightmares about that trip. She wakes up in the middle of the night, screaming, 'Give me back my glasses, you stupid monkeys!'"

"Silence!" the police chief bellowed. He motioned to his guard. "Lock them all up."

• • •

Jack's parents were put in the cell next to Jack and Harry.

"We'll have this straightened out with the chief in a jiff," his mom said.

Jack folded his arms. "You lied to the police."

"Apparently, wanting to find your son is a crime these days," Jack's dad said.

"We don't even know the laws in this country. We could end up with life sentences. We might even get hanged," Jack said.

"Just when I finally found myself," Harry muttered.

"Don't be silly, boys," Jack's mom said. "Nobody gets hanged over a mix-up. Oh! I almost forgot. I picked up our forwarded post yesterday. Jack, you got mail." She pulled a postcard out of her pocket and handed it through the bars.

The front of the card had a picture of a red-and-yellow Ferris wheel. The back read:

I got your letter. I hope you are having fun gnoming. Take good care of Mack and take lots of pictures of him. You can be in the pictures if you want. About the question you asked. Answer = yes.

Diana

Jack read it again. Answer equaled yes. He officially had a girlfriend. Now all he had to do was get out of jail so he could go on a date.

"Harry," Jack said. "Diana says she'll be my girlfriend."

"Awesome," Harry said. "Hopefully, your parents won't offer to take her to the mall and then end up accidentally losing her in the Congo."

Harry had been sitting in the corner of the cell, watching Jack's parents as if they were wild animals. "Dude, about our trade. My parents would love to have a kid like you around, but I can't subject them to these kinds of in-laws. I mean, my parents might not totally get who I am, but they're still my parents. I can't come home for Christmas and find out my mom and dad are spending the holidays in the slammer."

Jack nodded. He wasn't that surprised, but it was disappointing to learn Connecticut was definitely out. "That's okay, Harry. I hope we can still be friends."

"Absolutely," Harry said. "If you live to be eighteen, come find me. I'll make you a partner in the ice-cream business."

"Wait a minute," Jack's mom said. "What trade?"

"Oh," Jack said. "Harry and I were thinking about trading families. Harry is old enough to not need supervision, which would be great for you, and Harry's parents want a kid who wants to go to Harvard, which would be great for me. I figured you could help Harry launch his ice-cream business, while I stayed safe in Connecticut, working on my education. It seemed like a good fit."

"You were going to trade us in?" his mom said. "Like a car?" She turned and looked up to his dad. "Did you hear that, Richard? Traded in!"

"It's Nosnereb, isn't it?" Jack's dad asked. "You're not a fan. Just tell it to us straight, Jack. Your mom and I can think up a whole new religion. Any way you want it. I hear Wicca

131

is getting popular. We could always become witches."

"Good witches, obviously," his mom added.

"The problem isn't Nosnereb," Jack said. "Though I still think you can't just make up a religion. The reason I wanted to go to Connecticut is because nothing has changed. We've tried all these different things and what happened? 'Oh, look, Jack's lost again. Just another day in the life of the Berensons.'"

"Dude," Harry said. "You'll never change those two. My grandma says they've got the common sense of fruit bats."

Jack nodded. "I'm not even mad. I just feel hopeless."

Jack's mom gripped his dad's arm. "Hopeless is a bad sign, Richard. It would be better if Jack were furious, like he usually is."

Jack's dad patted his mom's hand and whispered, "I'll handle this." He leaned on the cell bars and said, "Now, Son, we have to insist on furious. Think of all the things you have to be furious about. Did we lose you once? No! Twice? No! We lost you three times! You don't have a reason in the world to be hopeless. Furious is the way to go."

Jack stared at his dad. No rules or lectures were ever going to change his parents.

"Jack," his mom said, "we tried so hard to do everything exactly the way you wanted."

"Keeping track of all the rules you wrote still makes my head hurt," his dad said.

"Don't trade us in," his mom added.

His parents *had* tried. Jack had to give them that. They hadn't been very successful, but there had been no lack of effort. Maybe it was time to stop trying to force his family into the picture he had invented in his head.

Before Jack had met Harry, he had been so sure that everybody else on the planet was living in a normal family. But Harry had been pressured to go to Harvard when all he wanted to do was sell ice cream. And worse, Harry's parents were disappointed in him for that reason. Maybe every family had its problems. Jack's family's problems were just more . . . noticeable.

Richard and Claire Berenson were highly

dangerous. There was no getting around that. But at least they were never disappointed in Jack.

The chief of police appeared in front of the cells, holding a piece of paper. His hand gripped the paper so hard that his fingers had turned white.

The chief stared at Richard and Claire Berenson. In a low voice, he said, "When you reported having seen two criminals wanted for a bank robbery, I contacted the Swiss Embassy to let them know we had a lead. I also reported it to my senior officer in Kathmandu. I have just received this response from my supervisor."

He held the paper in front of him and read:

"There has been no bank robbery in Switzerland. Is this some kind of joke? Send explanation at once."

"Oh, dear," Jack's mom said.

"I will be ruined," the chief said. "My entire family will be ruined."

"Wait a minute, sir," Jack said. "It wouldn't be fair for you to be ruined just because you met my parents. After all, they didn't mean to commit a crime. They just sometimes don't use very good judgment...And then end up committing a crime."

His mom nodded. "Listen to Jack. He knows how we are."

The chief stared at Jack's mom. He looked as if he wanted to reach through the bars and throttle her.

"You could always say that two foreigners came in to report the crime, but now they have disappeared," Jack said. "You think it might have something to do with . . . well, it might be . . ."

What would it have to do with? Jack didn't know anything about Nepal. The only thing he knew about the country was that it had been on strike.

"Maybe it had something to do with the strike?" he asked.

The chief whipped his head around to Jack. "The strike? The strike! Of course, the strike. Disruptions across the country...Why not false reports to the police? It would be unusual, of course. But not impossible." He paused, then said, "You would have to leave the country immediately."

"You mean, we'd have to go on the run?"
Jack asked.

"Just to the airport, Jack," his mom said.
"No worries, we've done it dozens of times."

* * *

Two hours later, the chief's brother-in-law
arrived with a pickup truck. The Berensons
and Harry were herded out a side entrance of
the police station and piled into the back of the
vehicle. Jack lay sandwiched between Harry and
his parents. Before the brother-in-law secured
a canvas tarp to the top of the truck bed, the
chief peered inside and said, "You will make no
stops. You will go directly to the airport. Take
the first flight out, no matter where it is going.
Do not ever come back."

As Jack bounced along under the tarp on
the road heading back toward Kathmandu, he
thought about what he would do when he got
home. Now that Connecticut was off the table,
he would be living with his parents again. And
his parents would have to find new jobs. But
who would hire them? To do what?

There had to be a way to make the Berenson family work. Jack had helped Harry figure out what to do with his life. There had to be something his own parents were good at.

"Harry," Jack said, "if my mom and dad took some of your parent's executive lambs on a trip, do you think the lambs would come back as executive lions?"

"If they came back at all, they'd come back with nerves of steel."

Harry was right. If there was one thing Jack's parents did well, it was toughen a person up.

Jack rolled over on his side and said to his mom and dad, "I've been trying so hard to turn you into people you're not. People you can't be no matter how hard you try. Maybe it's time to start using your natural strengths."

"So you're not trading us in?" his mom asked.

"I'm not trading you in," Jack said. "But it's time for you to get real jobs and keep them. And I know what those jobs are going to be."

Jack explained the executive training business. "You see, that way, when you accidentally lose an executive in some remote location—and you know you will—you can say that it was supposed to happen. It was part of the program. Your motto could be, 'Expect the unbelievable.'"

Jack's mom echoed him: "Expect the unbelievable."

Jack's dad rolled over on his side. "Son, I told your mum, 'Mark my words, that boy has got the Berenson brains.' You're a regular chip off the old block."

"Then it's settled," Jack said. "From now on, you just have to be yourselves. But you have to promise to work really hard at it."

"We will put our noses to the grindstone, Jack," his mom said.

"We'll grind our noses right off our faces if we have to," his dad said.

"We will work our fingers to the bone," his mom said.

"And then we'll keep on working, with just the bloody finger bones," his dad said.

"Okay," Jack said, "that's enough blood and bones and grindstones. I was just hoping you'd put in an eight-hour day."

"We can do that," his mom said. "Can't we, Richard?"

"Of course we can. After all, we *are* the Berensons."

Jack thought his dad had pretty much summed it up. He hadn't gotten the family of his dreams. His parents hadn't turned into the role models he had hoped for. They had stayed the Berensons, and they were never going to be anyone but the Berensons.

"The first thing we have to do," Jack said, "is get rid of that farmhouse in Shangrilala. I suppose since you bought it online, we could sell it online when we get home."

"Don't worry about the farmhouse," his dad said. "We've determined that the town of Shangrilala doesn't actually exist. That has led us to conclude that we purchased a farmhouse that doesn't exist."

"I told you Shangrilala didn't sound like a real town," Jack said.

"No more buying houses on the internet," his mom said. "Lesson learned."

•••

The first flight out of the airport was headed to Karachi. Jack and his parents spent two long days waiting for a connecting flight to the United States. Harry decided to stay behind in Pakistan and wait a week for the next one. He had told Jack's parents that he had met a man who knew how to make apple ice cream, and he was determined to get the recipe. And then he had told Jack privately that he had no intention of flying over the ocean with the Berensons on board. It was just too risky.

When Jack finally put his feet down on American soil, he got to work on his parent's new business plan.

CHAPTER 10

In which the Berensons play to their strengths

Jack smoothed his hair down and stared into the mirror. His dad had tied his tie for him. This was it. He was meeting Diana at the holiday dance. Everybody knew that meeting a girl at a dance was practically a first date. If he survived the night, then all he had to do was survive the actual holiday. Should he buy Diana a Christmas present? Did she get him something? If she had got him a gift, was it romantic or socks? Sometimes navigating middle school was harder than being lost in the wilderness.

At least Diana had finally got over what happened to Mack the monkey, though she still said Jack was irresponsible for letting it get attacked by so many wild animals. Jack had bought the monkey a sweatshirt and sunglasses to cover up its injuries. Mack was now confined to gnoming on Jack's bedroom bureau.

Jack had spent two months writing his parents' business plan and marketing their unique service. Now The Berenson Executive Training Company ("Expect the Unbelievable!") was a huge success. The media had been impressed that the program arranged to have a young corporate vice president disappear into the Ugandan jungle and get adopted by mountain gorillas. Park rangers found the man thirty pounds lighter than when he started, and the VP reported that it had been a "life-changing experience." Nobody but Jack understood that nothing had been arranged.

Harry had driven The Wandering Cone across the United States. When he hit California, he discovered surfing. He had called Jack to say that he sells cones when he's not catching waves.

His most popular flavor was the Chillax: swirled passion fruit and caramel.

Jack's mom popped her head around the doorframe. "Almost ready, luv?"

"Yup," he said, though Jack wasn't sure he would ever totally be ready to go on his first practically a date.

"Oh, by the way," his mom said, "pack a bag."

Jack spun around. "Pack a bag? Why? You're not taking me anywhere, are you?"

"Don't be a goose," his mom said. "Your father and I just received an emergency call from a large paper products company. The CEO wants his top executives to buck up, and he wants them to buck up fast."

Jack's dad appeared beside his mom. "So we said, consider it done."

"I've already spoken to Zack's mum, and you can stay with them until we get back from the Arctic Circle," his mom said.

Jack peered in the mirror and smoothed his hair one last time. "Take your warmest coats. And don't let anybody get eaten by a polar bear. And remember to wear your gloves. And don't let anybody float away on an iceberg. And bring long underwear. And don't hang around with seals; Orca whales will snatch you right off the beach."

"Don't worry, Jack," his mom said, "we know what we're doing."

"Finally," his dad said.

Jack supposed his mom was right; he shouldn't worry. His parents really did seem to know what they were doing. And anyway, Jack wasn't a top executive from a paper products company who was about to be lost at the North Pole. Jack was staying in Pennsylvania. He had no plans to leave the state until he drove himself to Harvard.

About the Author

Lisa Doan is the author of the Berenson Schemes series. She received a master's degree in writing for children and young adults from Vermont College of Fine Arts. Her travels in Africa and Asia and eight years spent living in the Caribbean were the basis for the series' international settings. She has hatched her share of schemes, including backpacking alone from Morocco to Kenya, hitchhiking across the Sahara, and opening a restaurant with no actual restaurant experience. Her occupations have included master scuba diving instructor, New York City headhunter, owner-chef of a 'Chinese-like' restaurant, television show set medic, and deputy prothonotary of a county court. Visit the author at lisadoan.org.

About the Illustrator

Ivica Stevanovic has illustrated picture books such as *The Royal Treasure Measure* and *Monsters Can Mosey*, as well as book covers and graphic novels. He also teaches classes at the Academy of Arts in Novi Sad, in northern Serbia. He lives in Veternik, northern Serbia, with his wife, Milica, who is also a children's illustrator, and their daughter, Katarina.